I, Survivor.

Andrew Yong

I, Survivor.

First edition trade paperback

Cover design by Sarah Elbert
Cover photo by Will Barratt

PER THE AUTHOR'S REQUEST, A PORTION OF ALL PROCEEDS FROM THIS BOOK WILL BE DONATED TO THE "HONEY ISLAND STRONG" FOUNDATION WHICH PROVIDES FINANCIAL SUPPORT AND CONTINUED PSYCHIATRIC TREATMENT FOR THE FAMILIES OF THE VICTIMS THAT PERISHED IN THE 2007 HONEY ISLAND SWAMP MASSACRE.

Table of Contents

"Goodnight kittens and goodnight mittens,
I miss you, Sabrina..."

INTRODUCTION

I was born on October 30, 1975, just one day short of being a Halloween baby. I'll never know what my unborn reasoning may have been but I decided to come into this world almost three full weeks before science said I was supposed to. It's a trait that I would carry with me for the rest of my natural life as I've always been one of those people who just can't help but show up early to wherever it is I may be going. Maybe it's a touch of OCD? Perhaps I'm just scared I might miss out on something? All I know is that my tendency to always be early started right out of the gate.

My mother used to say that my premature arrival was because I was anxious to get started saving the world. Something I always thought I was going to do when I grew up. Instead, I'd wind up living through one of the most horrific mass murders of all time, falsely accused of being the maniac that conducted it and vilified by the very world I wanted to save.

If only I had been late to work that day. Had I showed up just five minutes later, they likely would have left without me. But no, I was the first one there as usual. Just like my mother had always said, I was anxious to save the day.

Well, look at me now, Ma.

Top of the world.

Some might say that being the sole survivor of a brutal massacre makes me incredibly lucky, but ten years later I can assure you that surviving was, in fact, a curse. My reward for living through that terrible tragedy was to be strung up on the cross and eternally hated by the entire world. After all, society always needs someone to blame when the actual truth doesn't make sense.

I can't blame the world for hating me. Had I not been the one to witness what really happened I wouldn't believe my story either. However, just like the multiple polygraph tests that I've passed over the years have shown you, every word you're about to read is true and I will stand by the truth for the rest of this life and the next.

The fundamental problem in all of this is that while I may have been acquitted by a grand jury and cleared of every single atrocious crime I was accused of, it will never be enough to convince anyone that I didn't actually commit those horrific murders. To the general population, my acquittal does not mean that I am innocent. It only means that the prosecution didn't have enough evidence to convict me.

Believe me, I know the score.

While I don't expect this book to change the world's collective opinion of me, I do hope that just maybe these pages will finally give me the chance to thoroughly explain what really happened and who I really am.

I never hurt anyone.

The only thing I did wrong was survive.

I wish to god every day that I hadn't.

Chapter One

The Beginning

On June 30, 1973, an 18-year-old boy named Jen-Hsun Yong met a 17-year-old girl named Anna Lee Kao at a local ice cream parlor in Kissimmee, Florida where they both lived at the time.

Like a scene from a Hollywood romantic comedy, Jen-Hsun was actually driving out of the parking lot when he spotted Anna walking into the ice cream shop. Apparently, Cupid hit Jen-Hsun hard enough with his arrow to get him to stop his car and run back inside. Pretending that he hadn't just finished eating ice cream mere *moments* beforehand, Jen-Hsun smoothly saddled up next to Anna at the counter and nonchalantly ordered ice cream cones for both of them.

It's important to note that Anna had already seen Jen-Hsun leaving the ice cream shop and therefore knew that he had purposely come back in and sat back down at the counter just to get a chance to speak to her.

It's even *more* important to note that Jen-Hsun was already on a date with another girl and that he left her waiting in the car while he ate ice cream with Anna and got her phone number.

My parents would be married less than one year later.

As adorable as the story may be for how my mother and father met, their rushed marriage was more out of necessity and less out of whirlwind romance.

My mother was already three months pregnant when she and my father tied the knot.

As fate would have it, however, my mother lost the baby just a few weeks after the wedding. At that point it would have been relatively easy for Jen-Hsun and Anna to play their virtual "get out of jail free" cards and go their separate ways had they wanted to. Instead they began trying to get pregnant again right away.

They had been married just over one year when I arrived.

In modern times where marriage has become more like "going steady" and where divorce has become an easy out for far too many couples, getting married so young would almost certainly spell disaster. Not my parents though. They defied the odds and stayed together.

I've often wondered what it would have been like if my brother or sister had lived. Given that my parents never had another child after me, I'm not so sure that I would even exist. My mother's miscarriage was a very difficult subject for my parents and they never discussed it with me again after the day they first explained it to me. Given my lack of social life growing up, I often fantasized about having a sibling to play with. Would my childhood have been more fun with an older brother or sister? Or would competing for my parents' undivided attention and affection have only made things harder for me?

I'll never know for sure.

Shortly after getting married my parents relocated to Baton Rouge, Louisiana where my father found work as an auto mechanic and my mother worked part-time as the secretary in a dentist's office. Money may have been tight but they never let it show and I rarely remember a time where I had to go without.

Looking back now, the fact that we had pancakes for dinner at least twice a week always felt like a treat to me and less like what it really was, which was my folks struggling to get through until the next paycheck.

Not only were there no siblings for me to play with, I had no extended family to speak of either. Both of my father's parents and my grandmother on my mom's side had all passed away before I was born and while I've seen photographs of my mother's father holding me as an infant, he sadly died of lung cancer shortly after my first birthday.

According to my mother, my grandfather had always been the epitome of good health. He ran two miles every morning, he was a vegetarian long before the dietary lifestyle became common, and he never smoked a single cigarette in his entire life.

One day he woke up with pains in his chest and a nasty cough. He went to the doctor fearing he may have come down with bronchitis and instead received a death sentence of inoperable lung cancer.

Seven weeks later he was dead at age 52.

Asian people may statistically live long lives but unfortunately in my family the opposite is true.

The few relatives that I knew of all lived in China and I often got the impression that my parents had been kind of kicked out of the clan due to my mother's teenage pregnancy and subsequent "shotgun wedding." What's ironic is that supposedly my uncles and aunts were all divorced yet they still looked down at my parents for getting pregnant before they were married. My folks may have been the black sheep of their families but if there was ever a shining example of the perfect marriage, it was Jen-Hsun and Anna Yong.

Years later when my own marriage would hit hard times I asked my father what the secret to a good marriage was.

"The secret is this," he said. "Every morning, the first thought that goes through both of your heads needs to be '*what can I do today to help make my partner's day a little easier?*' Not '*what can my partner do to help me?*' If you both instinctively put each other's happiness before your own then you are an unstoppable and unbreakable team."

While I stand by my father's words and would give any new couple that exact same advice, the key to the equation is that you *both* need to think the same way in order for it to work. Not just one of you.

Time would eventually teach me that painful lesson.

When I was fifteen years old my parents informed me that I actually had a cousin from my mother's side of the family that lived in the States. At first I was angry that they had kept this information from me but once they explained the entire situation I quickly understood why.

Apparently my cousin had grown up in Dallas where he had joined a gang by the time he was just fourteen years old. He had spent his entire life in and out of prison and his criminal record included everything from armed robbery to domestic battery and sexual assault. The way they spoke about this guy you would have thought they were talking about the devil himself.

My cousin's name was Dingbang. No joke, *Dingbang*. Clearly, my aunt and uncle had a different kind of lifestyle in mind for my cousin when they named him since Dingbang means "protector of the country" in Chinese. While Dingbang may have been an honorable name in China, in America they may as well have named him "Douchebag." Perhaps Dingbang was just revolting against his given name by becoming a full-on pariah and it is really all my aunt and uncle's fault that he turned out so rotten?

Somewhere along the way, Dingbang had changed his name to "Bang." The only reason my parents told me about him at all was because Bang had reportedly relocated to the New Orleans area and they feared that he may seek us out and turn up at our house one day.

That day never happened. As far as I know, these days Bang is either dead or in prison but I'll never know for sure.

My earliest memories were cartoons and comic books. I loved all of the superheroes. Literally *all* of them. The concept that there were regular human beings bestowed with special powers who used their gifts to help others and save the day in the nick of time meant everything to me.

While it may seem obvious that I would grow up to become a paramedic and help save lives given how enamored I was with superheroes, the truth was that I originally wanted to be a comic book writer.

I used to daydream in class that I was the Asian American version of Stan Lee with my own empire of comic creations that would rival those of both Marvel and D.C. Comics combined. However, I didn't have the kind of artistic skill it would take to make a career out of comics. To this day anything I draw that isn't a smiling sun wearing sunglasses is utterly indecipherable.

Thankfully I would discover a new all-consuming passion when I was just ten years old.

Music.

Call it hair metal, glam metal, cock rock, garbage, or whatever you want, I was fortunate enough to grow up in the greatest decade for music in all of history. The 1980's will never be rivaled.

I remember exactly where I was the first time I heard *Poison's* "Talk Dirty To Me." It was February 1987 and I was at a flea market with my mother. We were at a table with various Tupperware (or I should say flimsy Tupperware knockoffs known as "Supper-ware" as it was a flea market after all) and the woman with the big hair working behind the table had a grey boombox tuned to a local radio station. From the moment C.C. Deville's opening guitar lick blasted from her boom box, time froze for me. They may not be the most revered or celebrated band in music, but hearing *Poison* for the first time was like being hit by a bolt of lightning.

I got my mom to take me to the record store that same day and despite her reservations over what the band looked like (she was convinced that *Poison* was made up of four incredibly homely women), she bought me the single. A little 45 record with "Talk Dirty To Me" on Side A and "Want Some, Need Some" on Side B. I still have it in my record collection to this day.

I knew right then and there that I was going to move to Los Angeles, put on make-up, and be in a huge rock band.

It would still be another four years before we got cable in our house, but thankfully our neighbors could afford it. I must have spent 10-15 hours every week watching MTV at the MacKenzie's home.

I'll admit I was really just using Kevin MacKenzie. I was pretending to be friends with him just so that I could watch MTV whenever I could. Kevin's parents were both chain smokers and though my eyes would literally burn from the thick cloud of cancer that filled the inside of their home, it was worth it just to be able to watch music videos.

Kevin was a weird kid that seemed to have an aversion to bathing and always smelled like he had peed his pants. Among his collection of toys were five different *Cabbage Patch Kid* dolls and several *Barbie* dolls. A bit odd for a boy (most of the boys my age played with *Star Wars* action figures, *Transformers*, or *G.I. Joe's*) but Kevin had every single *M.A.S.K.* action figure and vehicle so I was at least able to find some common ground to help pull off my friendship charade with him. Then again, I was willing to play with whatever toys Kevin wanted to play with so long as we played in front of his living room television and I could watch MTV.

Kevin had adopted the nickname "Spuds" after Budweiser's party dog mascot "Spuds MacKenzie" who was featured in their commercials for a long run in the late 80's.

When you look back at the concept now, the whole "Spuds MacKenzie" thing was seriously gross. I'd love to have been a fly on the wall in the marketing meeting when some genius executive pitched the concept of a Bull Terrier that loved to party and that women couldn't resist.

Rather than question the absurdity of the concept or raise a few dozen red flags about the subliminal promotion of bestiality that Budweiser's commercials were celebrating, someone in charge at Anheuser-Busch said "brilliant," the world embraced "Spuds

MacKenzie," and the partying dog became somewhat of a cultural icon.

A few little-known facts about "Spuds MacKenzie": the concept was the brainchild of a 23-year-old art director named Jon Moore. "Spuds" first appeared in a commercial during Superbowl XXI where the New York Giants defeated the Denver Broncos 39 to 20 and won their first Superbowl since 1957.

Though "Spuds" would become an instant hit with plush toys and T-shirts in stores across the country, once it was revealed that "Spuds" was actually a female dog "his" career started to come under fire and unravel.

If you think about it (which apparently I have), it makes sense that they would cast a female dog to portray "Spuds" as it's not like Budweiser would have been able to use footage of a Bull Terrier participating in conga lines and holding on to half-naked women with a raging red-rocket lipstick erection.

Eventually, the social justice warriors of the time came after Anheuser-Busch with allegations that they were using "Spuds" to appeal to children and get them interested in Budweiser beer at an impressionable young age.

Laugh all you want, but just look at Kevin. He was a young boy that adopted the nickname "Spuds" and then grew up to become a full-blown alcoholic who would eventually drink himself to death. Kevin died of liver failure at the age of 32.

"Spuds" (whose real name was "Honey Tree Evil Eye", no shit) was forced into retirement in 1989 and sadly passed away from renal failure in 1993.

Rest in peace, "Spuds."

Both of you.

During those after-school play sessions at the MacKenzie's, I would study the videos on the television and pick them apart frame by frame. Back home in my bedroom at night I would stand in front of the mirror and imitate the way Jon Bon Jovi smiled at the girls, the way David Lee Roth effortlessly threw out ninja kicks, the way Dee Snider sneered at authority figures, the way W. Axl Rose dangerously slithered behind his microphone, the way David Coverdale shoved his tongue down Tawny Kitain's throat, and the way Kip Winger magically played his bass guitar without ever seeming to actually touch it.

Those were the days of *quality* music. Songs were songs and men were men… who looked like women.

Don't get me wrong. I still planned on saving the world. Only it wouldn't be as a masked superhero wearing spandex. It would be as a sexually androgynous rock n roll hero wearing spandex.

And glitter.

Lots and lots of glitter.

Growing up in Baton Rouge and being one of only two Asian American kids in my class made school hell for me. There were plenty of other Asian Americans in the city of Baton Rouge but for some unfortunate reason, my particular graduating class suffered from a significant shortage of kids that looked like me.

Back then being bullied was considered a rite of passage and something that every kid was almost expected to go through as they made their way through adolescence. I was called names like "Ching Chong Yong," "Slant Eyed Andy," and my personal favorite "Yong Fried Rice."

Believe it or not, it was my gym teacher Mr. Reynolds who came up with that last gem. The first time he called me "Yong Fried Rice" during kickball it got such a big laugh from the rest of the class that he called me by that racist nickname for the next three years and beat his shitty joke so far into the ground that it went all the way to… *China.*

Get it? All the way to *China?*

I can make that joke because I'm Chinese. But if you laughed at it and you're not Chinese…congratulations, you're a racist. Shame on you!

I'm kidding, of course.

Believe it or not, I actually have a sense of humor about that kind of stuff. I believe there's a fine line between *joking* about our differences and actual *racism.*

Speaking of…

How do you know a Chinese man robbed your home? Your homework is done and your computer is upgraded but two hours later the dude is still trying to back out of your driveway.

I'm sure the publisher is going to edit that last part out if my writing partner doesn't edit it out first. Hey Joe, leave it in okay?

These days a teacher like Mr. Reynolds would be instantly fired for joking with a student in such a manner but when I was in school it was considered par for the course. Sadly, my own bullying didn't end with the ignorant name-calling. There were many instances where I was physically hurt by the assholes at school that got some kind of sadistic joy out of beating up on the little Asian kid that was half their size.

It sucked to look different. To know that in every class photo I instantly stuck out like a sore thumb because of the shape of my eyes. It didn't make a difference that I was born in the United States and had grown up in Baton Rouge just like every other kid in my class. I looked different and therefore I could never quite feel accepted.

Even worse than the awful nicknames and the occasional bruises that I'd hide from my parents was how my Chinese heritage massively limited my chances with the opposite sex. As I mentioned there was one other Asian American kid in my class.

Her name was Jennifer Chen and her parents had moved from Hong Kong to Baton Rouge the summer before 2nd grade. What followed was a decade of Jennifer and I being forced to pair up whenever the situation called for it. A school project that required partners? "Andrew and Jennifer, you'll be working together." After-school activities like drama club? "Andrew and Jennifer, you'll be auditioning for the roles of 'Kenickie' and 'Rizzo' together… but you'll never get the parts because *Grease* is only for white kids and everyone knows that."

The absolute worst were the school dances. By default, Jennifer and I were automatically each other's dates. Our options were to go with each other, go alone, or stay home.

Jennifer was a beautiful girl. She was brilliant and fiercely competitive. She could play the violin like Sayaka Katsuki. (She's a very famous violinist.) We got along fine but we just weren't each other's type.

You see, for all of grade school I had my eyes on someone else.

Stacey Mazzoli was a gorgeous Italian girl who came from a huge Sicilian family. Sophomore year I finally gathered up the nerve to ask Stacey to the Homecoming dance.

Much to my surprise she said "yes!"

Sadly, the very next day she broke it to me that her parents wouldn't allow her to go to the dance with me. In the words of her father, "you'll break your Nana's heart if she finds out you're going to a dance with a chink."

Ouch.

I skipped the homecoming dance entirely. I lied to my parents and said that I wasn't feeling well just to save myself the embarrassment of admitting that I couldn't find a date. While all of the other kids in my class were at the dance I was at home in my bedroom listening to records and practicing my stage moves in the mirror.

Skid Row's first album had become my go-to record whenever I would lip-sync performances in my bedroom mirror. I would pretend that I was on stage in a massive stadium like I saw in music videos and I would just disappear into the love and adoration of the imaginary crowd that stretched out before me.

There was a song on Side 2 of that first *Skid Row* record called "I Remember You" that I would play over and over again. I'd pretend that I could effortlessly hit every high note that Sebastian Bach belted out while I emoted every lyric of a love lost.

I don't know which was sadder, the fact that I was pretending that I'd ever be able to sing like Sebastian Bach or the fact that I was lip-syncing a love song over and over again yet I had no idea what love was and had never even come close to feeling it.

The night of the homecoming dance I'm pretty sure I put on the best show of my imaginary career.

Later that very same night I had an incredibly vivid dream that I was holding a girl's hand. I couldn't see her face, I could only look down and see her hand in mine. The dream seemed to go on for hours and I was perfectly fine with that. I didn't want to wake up and have it be over. I never forgot the dream because it felt so real. In my dreams I usually don't feel anything at all. But that night I could literally feel every curve of this girl's hand. It was so real that I could still feel her touch for the first few minutes after I had woken up.

I would have that same dream at least a dozen more times over the next few years but I could never see the girl's face. All I could see was her hand in mine.

The hand belonged to a black girl.

Over the years I learned to forgive Stacey Mazzoli for not standing up to her racist father, but at the time it was absolutely soul crushing. After Stacey backed out of going to the dance with me I was embarrassed to be in my own skin. I felt like some kind of monster. I'd look in the mirror and only see "ugly." I was ashamed of who I was, so much so that I never attended a school dance again. I officially gave up and withdrew socially.

I spent all of my free time alone listening to records and plotting my career as a rock star. Someday *I'd* be the one with a video on MTV. I'd be so famous that I would be able to have any girl that I wanted.

Even Stacey Mazzoli if I still so desired.

While rejection may serve as fuel for many artists, the truth is that it also leaves deep scars that never entirely heal.

Years later when I would be facing the death penalty for multiple crimes that I did not commit I'd strangely realize that I actually had something in common with the monster that *did* commit those atrocious crimes.

We had both been bullied and ostracized by society for looking different. It may seem impossible but as I stood there in court defending my life I actually had great sympathy in my heart for him.

Despite all of the pain and suffering he has caused for so many (myself included) I still pity him even today.

I was sixteen when I decided that I was going to pursue a career as a paramedic. It happened in a crashing instant.

Literally.

My mother was driving me to the dentist when we witnessed a terrible accident that ended one man's life and changed my own.

We were slowing down for a red light at an intersection when a man on a motorcycle decided to gun it past us and blow right through the light.

It all happened so fast. I remember being startled by the sound of his motorcycle as it screamed past my window into the intersection. The light turned red and half a second later I watched in horror as he was T-boned by a car that had jumped the gun into the intersection.

The impact sounded like an explosion in a war movie. It was as if someone had fired a cannon just fifteen feet away from my ears.

The motorcycle and the man riding it were pinned to the front of the car when it slammed head first into a tree.

The sound was absolutely sickening.

I froze in my seat but my brave mother jumped into action immediately.

"Stay here, Andrew," she ordered.

A moment later she was taking charge of the scene, giving out orders to other witnesses, and calmly asking for someone to call 911.

She never even raised her voice.

She just took control.

I had always known that my mother was an incredibly strong woman but watching the way she stoically handled the emergency proved to me that she was indeed one of the strongest women in the entire world.

Thankfully, from my position inside of the car I couldn't see the motorcyclist's body pinned between the car and the tree. But once the blood began to puddle up in the street I knew that there was no possible way that he had survived the accident.

I wanted so badly to get out of the car and help but I was frozen to my seat in fear.

I remember thinking "what would Superman do right now?"

Where was my courage?

But that's the thing about courage.

You might *think* you're brave.

You might *want* to help.

You might *wish* you could save the day.

But until the moment of truth arises you never know what you're really made of.

My mother was taking control of the horrible situation and doing everything she could to help, yet I couldn't even find the strength to unbuckle my seat belt.

I was paralyzed.

Useless.

A few minutes later when the police, fire trucks, and paramedics had arrived my mother gave her statement and calmly got back in the car.

"Is he gonna be okay?" I asked.

"No," she answered. "There was nothing anyone could have done to save him."

She put her hand on my shoulder. "Are *you* okay?"

I whispered "yes" but my head was uncontrollably shaking "no."

"How did you do that?" I stammered. "How were you not too scared to help?"

I began to sob. Mostly out of sadness for the man who had just died right in front of me but also out of shame for myself. After so many years of dreaming about being a superhero, when push actually came to shove I had folded like a deck chair.

I was nothing but a coward.

"Do you know what Yong means in Chinese, Andrew?" My mother asked me.

I blinked back at her, confused. "No."

"Yong means *hero*," she answered.

Some hero I was.

I couldn't help but wonder about the man on the motorcycle. When he woke up that morning did he have the slightest idea that he was going to die that day? Did he get to say goodbye to his family? What was the last thing he said to his girlfriend? Or his wife? Or his children?

Oh god, did he have children?

What was it going to be like for his own mother when she got the phone call from the police informing her that her son was dead?

I vowed at that moment to never again freeze up in the face of tragedy. Never again would I be the one to hide while others did whatever they could do to help.

I thought long and hard about the massive relief I felt once the ambulance had finally shown up and the EMT's had taken control of the scene.

I wanted to be the person that made everyone feel better when I showed up.

I wanted to live up to my family name.

I wanted to be a *hero*.

I wanted to be an EMT.

My parents supported my career epiphany, however, they insisted that I graduate from a four-year college with a nursing degree and not just take the necessary courses to become a certified EMT.

I know that they secretly hoped that nursing school would possibly lead to me becoming a nurse or a doctor but I wanted to be the guy who showed up on the scene of a terrible motorcycle accident and saved the day.

I wanted to be on the front lines.

I wanted to be the one who answered the call for help.

The following Fall I applied to the University of Louisiana Lafayette's nursing program. I'll never forget the look of pride on my mother and father's faces when I opened the envelope and saw that I had indeed been accepted.

Accepted.

The word meant so much more to me than just getting into college.

Though I now had a purpose and a path for my life after High School, I still had to get through the rest of my dreadful senior year. At least now there was a shining light at the end of the dark tunnel.

As I retreated further into social isolation my book covers became filled with my scribbled song lyrics and logos for the various band names I would come up with. You would think that I would have picked up an instrument in my free time but I always knew I would be a lead singer.

I couldn't really sing very well but that never stopped me from dreaming big.

Over the years I've had many almost-bands that were really just names and logos:

- *Ice Scream*
- *Faucethead*
- *Yongulation*
- *Cry Beer*
- *Howling Yonder*
- *Baton Rouge*

Coincidentally, the name *Baton Rouge* would be made semi-famous by another band from the area. In 1990 *Baton Rouge* released their debut record "Shake Your Soul" and their song "Walks Like A Woman" got about ten minutes of radio play before disappearing into obscurity.

I formed *Cry Beer* with kids I met from a nearby vocational school. We had a few rehearsals and learned a few cover songs but we never played any shows publicly as we disbanded before any gigs could happen.

I still believe *Yongulation* could have been a contender. For that one I recruited three freshmen that were playing in the school band. I spent two months designing our logo but by the time I finished, graduation was looming and I was about to leave for college, so the band broke up before we ever played together. It's a shame as our logo was incredible.

As sad as I was to see *Yongulation* dissolve so early in its infancy, I couldn't have been happier to see High School end.

I left Baton Rouge for Lafayette at the end of summer and I never looked back. Lafayette may physically only be about an hour and fifteen-minute drive away from Baton Rouge, but as far as I was concerned it may as well have been on the other side of the world. UL Lafayette was an entirely new start for me and I was overjoyed to get away from my hometown and the people I had grown up with.

Wanting to make the most of my college experience I opted for on-campus housing my freshman year. I was assigned a roommate named Howard and thankfully we got along great. I may have despised his rap music and he definitely loathed my beloved hair metal, but we had most everything else in common. I felt like I had finally made a real friend but sadly it wasn't meant to last.

For financial reasons that he never fully explained, Howard suddenly dropped out of school after just six weeks. I was despondent to see him go, but having a double room to myself for the rest of that first semester was pretty incredible.

When the second semester started I was once again assigned a new roommate.

We'll just refer to him as Lord Asshole.

Lord Asshole was nothing like Howard. He was such a slob that he never washed or changed his bed sheets for the entire semester. Keep in mind this is college. So you can only imagine some of the foul things that drunkenly happened on his cesspool of a bed.

When I finally got up the nerve to say something about the horrible smell of his sheets his response was to hang a few "Little Tree" vanilla-roma car fresheners around our room with middle fingers drawn on them.

The worst aspect of Lord Asshole wasn't his lack of cleanliness though. He was a terrible drunk that would always want to argue with anyone in his path after just a few beers. It didn't matter what the subject of the argument was, he just wanted to have a verbal fight every single time he drank.

If I said "up", Lord Asshole said "down."
If I said "black", Lord Asshole said "white."

If you've ever had to try and co-exist with a roommate that you despise then you know just how negatively it affects your entire life. Your bedroom should be your safe spot and a place of peace. The fact that I spent every night dreading going back to my room was no way to live and I found myself spending time almost anywhere *but* in my own room.

I spent most of my second semester in the library. If the library happened to be closed I would read or study in the dormitory's laundry room. When the weather was nice I would sit outside and study. I literally only went back to my room to sleep. It was terrible but at least my grades excelled from all of that studying.

In some ways, I need to thank Lord Asshole. I had been so focused on my classes that first year of college that I had completely put my goal of having a band on the back burner. Hating being in my dorm room for the entire second half of my freshmen year lead to my decision to answer a bulletin board flier for a local band seeking a new lead singer. I figured that even in a worst-case scenario, auditioning would give me a place to go for an evening.

Or just maybe I'd finally find the band I had been looking for all of my life.

I didn't know what to expect when I walked into the band's rehearsal space for the first time. When I called and set up my audition with the guitar player he didn't tell me too much about the band, not even their name. All he told me was that they had an old *Van Halen* sound and that they had already gained a small but loyal following by playing nightclubs several nights a month in and around the Lafayette area.

When I arrived at their jam space the first thing I noticed was the giant banner with the band's name on it hanging behind their backline of amplifiers.

Haddonfield.

Eventually, I would learn that the drummer and the guitarist were both big slasher movie fans and that *Haddonfield* was the name of the fictitious Illinois town where the 1978 movie *Halloween* had been set. The name never meant much to me as I just thought it sounded cool. Their logo was almost as cool as the one I had created for *Yongulation* and their evil jack-o-lantern mascot "Jack" reminded me of *Iron Maiden's* iconic "Eddie."

Had I known that one day I would be put on trial for allegedly committing a massacre I may have never joined *Haddonfield* as the prosecution had a field day attacking my character over the fact that I was in a band named after a popular slasher franchise. It didn't make a difference that I myself never even saw *Halloween* since I have never found anything enjoyable about watching horror films. My band's name would still be used against me in the fight of my life.

By the time I joined *Haddonfield* my original spandex and glitter-clad vision for a band had altered itself to change with the times… but only *slightly*. There would still be stage make-up involved just not as much as there would have been before rock music completely changed.

Just three years earlier on September 24, 1991, *Nirvana* had fired a shot across the bow of glam rock with the release of their second record "Nevermind" and suddenly all of the bands that I loved were playing on borrowed time if not extinct. Almost overnight, Seattle's grunge/alternative scene became the new mainstream style of rock music.

To me, grunge was merely the ugly stepchild of glam rock. Rock music that had once defined itself with a combination of highly polished operatic singing, technically proficient guitar solos, larger than life showmanship, and catchy, fun choruses that everyone could sing along to was replaced by a purposely sloppy sound, comically depressing lyrics, and band members that were trying *way* too hard to look like they didn't give a shit about what they looked like.

I mean, if you don't want to be a rock star then why be a rock star?

The alternative/grunge bands tried so hard to be the opposite of glam that they would even purposely use out of focus photos of themselves for the back cover of their records. It was as if they were saying "we don't care *so much* that even our photographer couldn't be bothered focusing the camera lens."

Grunge bands would try and tell you that they did away with lavish guitar solos in their songs because "guitar solos are lame" but the truth is that most lead guitarists in grunge bands just weren't capable of playing a decent solo.

Very few of the singers from the grunge bands had anything special about their voices and vocally they couldn't even come close to the breathtaking range that was an absolute requirement in glam rock.

I know that my opinion on 90's rock music is an unpopular one but I think that a significant reason why grunge became so popular so fast was that it made everyone feel like they could do it too.

Just think about it for a minute. The average guy can get on stage during karaoke and sing every note of a *Pearl Jam* song and sound pretty damn close to Eddie Vedder but very few guys on this planet can even attempt to sing the chorus of a *Cinderella* song and sound remotely close to Tom Keifer.

90's grunge/alternative music was merely the punk version of 80's glam metal as now musicians with extremely average talent could play heavy metal. Kurt Cobain couldn't hold a candle to Sebastian Bach vocally (incidentally, at one point Cobain had named his own band *Skid Row* before settling on the name *Nirvana*) and it was typical for a lead singer in a grunge band to miserably stand in one place for an entire set and act like it was a burden for them to even be on stage. If Jon Bon Jovi would fly over the audience on wires during *Bon Jovi* concerts then Layne Staley would just brood on his knees and not even look at the audience during *Alice In Chains* shows.

When you look back now, grunge is just as ridiculous as glam was in its own pretentious way. Bands went platinum by acting like they didn't want their careers. Concerts that used to be extravagant celebrations of sex, drugs, and rock n roll became sad gatherings of misery and angst. I understood bands dropping the teased hair and androgynous stage clothes as that shtick could only be considered cool for so long but now we were going to shows to watch bands scowl at us in T-shirts and jeans. Rock and roll… I guess?

Please don't think I'm bitter about grunge because I'm really not. Sure, the trend may have killed off a ton of the bands I loved but every style of music has its phase at the top of the mainstream before the masses grow tired of it and vote with their wallets to replace it with whatever scene is next in line to be beaten to death. If it hadn't been grunge that killed off all of the Sunset Strip glam metal bands it would have been something else.

I personally loved most of the grunge bands and I still think that records like *Alice In Chains'* "Jar Of Flies" and *Soundgarden's* "Bad Motorfinger" are absolute masterpieces. I'm just calling grunge bands out for what they so obviously were; a discount version of the truly great 80's bands that came before them.

Personally, I need to *thank* the grunge/alternative scene of the early 90's as it was precisely what made it possible for a mediocre singer like me to front a band without being humiliated.

My own vocal range is pretty limited so in many ways, I might never have gotten the gig with *Haddonfield* had the same standards of musicianship that were so popular in the 80's still been in style when I auditioned. There's a good chance that if I had met the guys in *Haddonfield* just three years earlier or three years later I may not have fit the bill.

I wish I could tell you more about each of the guys in the band but unfortunately, all four of them asked to not have their names mentioned anywhere in this book. To add insult to injury I'm not even allowed to mention any of the bars, nightclubs, or larger venues that I performed in with *Haddonfield* per the request of said establishments. Sadly, my name has become such mud that these people and places think that merely being associated with me is equivalent to slander.

If you ever want to find out who your real friends are, just get yourself falsely accused of committing one of the worst mass murders in history and watch how few of them actually stand by you.

It was years after I was exonerated and found innocent of all accusations across the board that I privately heard from each of the guys in *Haddonfield* again. The guys individually called me and apologized for turning their backs on me when I needed all of the support and character witnesses that I could possibly get to testify in my defense.

They may have apologized to me *off* the record many years after the fact but they still want nothing to do with me publicly.

And that, ladies and gentlemen, is the true brotherhood of a band.

For the purposes of this book, I'll only refer to my band-mates by the instruments they played.

Haddonfield's rehearsal space was located on the unfinished third story of an office building that was owned by the bass player's father. The space was massive, which was great for sound, and not having to pay rent for a rehearsal space was incredibly fortunate. The band could only practice after 7pm and on weekends when the various businesses on the first two floors were closed.

Only being able to practice at night was never an issue, but the lack of air conditioning certainly was. They had set up a few industrial sized fans but in the heat of the Louisiana summer all the fans really did was blow the hot air around. Moving the drummer's kit and the amplifiers up and down three stories of stairs every time there was a gig was pretty miserable but the guys had it down to a science and could fully load and unload the gear in less than 30 minutes.

From the moment that I walked into their rehearsal space, it was evident that the guitarist was the leader of the band. He and the bass player couldn't have been more welcoming to me, which was immensely appreciated for a shy guy like myself that was about to have to sing in front of strangers.

The drummer was pretty standoffish and didn't say much to me. I couldn't help but notice that he polished off about eight or nine beers in the two hours I was there. The rest of us each had a beer or two but the drummer was a heavy drinker who didn't even bother putting his personal 12-pack in the refrigerator. He could drink faster if he kept his beers directly beside his drum kit and he didn't care if they were cold or warm. His affinity for alcohol was something that would prove to be a major problem for *Haddonfield* later down the line and he would ultimately be shown the door and replaced just about a year later.

We spent the better part of the first hour talking about the bands that we liked and who our influences were. As I looked at the various band posters hung up around their rehearsal space I knew I was in the right place. *Van Halen, Guns N Roses, Aerosmith, Metallica, Tesla, Whitesnake…* these were my people for sure.

Eventually, the guys began to casually plug in and take their places around the room. I suddenly got incredibly nervous as I realized my actual audition was about to start… and I had never auditioned for a band before.

When I had attempted to put together bands in high school I had always been the one instigating everything so I had automatically had the role of lead singer in each of my failed attempts. This time I was the guest in someone else's house and I was going to have to prove that I belonged.

No pressure.

Most bands rehearse facing each other in somewhat of a circle but *Haddonfield* always rehearsed in show formation with everyone facing forward and playing for an imaginary crowd. The fact that I wouldn't have to face them while I sang gave me a massive boost of confidence.

Haddonfield didn't really bother with cover songs and already had a dozen original songs written when I met them but for audition purposes, we would be playing songs that we all knew.

The bass player launched into *Aerosmith's* "Sweet Emotion" (a standard for most cover bands) and I faced forward and imagined the mirror from my high school bedroom. “Sweet Emotion” was the one *Aerosmith* song that I knew I could sing well as it’s one of the few songs where Steven Tyler keeps his voice within the same range and doesn’t jump octaves or do anything with his signature high-pitched scream.

From there we played *Black Sabbath’s* “Paranoid” and *Guns N Roses* “Mr. Brownstone.”

They were an *incredibly* tight band with the bass and drums staying right in the pocket on every song and the guitarist showing off just how technically proficient he was as he flawlessly added his own brand of pull-offs and hammer-ons. It was as if he was singing through his guitar.

I knew right away that this was the band I had always dreamed of being in.

When the three cover songs were finished the guitarist handed me a notebook with lyrics in it.

“Just listen for a minute,” he said.

The band launched into one of their originals called “Something I Need” with the guitarist singing lead vocals. I followed along in the notebook as I listened.

I knew that they wouldn't have handed me an original song to try unless they had liked what they heard me do with the cover songs so my confidence was soaring. With cheesy lyrics like *"you never show no mercy, I like the way you talk"* I also knew that I'd be able to help elevate whatever originals they had already written. I couldn't wait to bring in my own books of lyrics and bring my own songs to life with them.

I did my best to belt out the song. I came in late on two of the verses but other than that I mostly pulled it off. We played it a second time and I really let loose adding some high screams to the final two choruses of the song. When we finished I turned around and I could see that they were all smiling.

I was in the band.

As my freshmen year came to a close I was playing shows with *Haddonfield* at least once or twice every two weeks, I was doing well in my classes, and overall I loved my life at UL Lafayette.

Except of course for my living situation with Lord Asshole.

That was definitely going to have to change before my sophomore year started and after a year of living in the dorms, I was ready for a substantial change of pace anyway.

To be honest, life in the dorms was too reminiscent of High School. You take a bunch of 18-year-old kids and put them all together in a dormitory where they'll be living away from the rules of their parents for the first time in their lives and it brings out the worst in far too many of them.

Almost every morning someone had thrown up in the bathroom. Parties raged deep into the night, music blared in the hallways whenever I was trying to sleep, and since most 18-year-olds can't handle their liquor there was never a shortage of fistfights. It was fairly typical for the campus' Public Safety officers to be called into my dorm to break up an altercation.

I was going to have to live elsewhere.

The very first place I looked at was a small studio apartment just about 20-30 minutes away from campus. It was about the size of a shoebox but it was only ten minutes away from *Haddonfield's* rehearsal space and yet still close enough to UL Lafayette to not be *too* much of an inconvenience commuting back and forth to campus for my classes.

As it turned out, I wound up being the very first person to view the apartment after it had been listed for rent. The landlord liked me, I said "yes," and my parents wired me the deposit that same day. It all worked out so quickly and perfectly that it felt like fate.

I moved into my new apartment in the city of Crowley, LA.

Chapter Two

The Meeting

The average college student enjoys having a few months off from school to reconnect with their friends and family back in whatever town or city they call "home" but I wanted no part in any of that so I signed up for three summer classes instead. My parents were disappointed that I wouldn't be coming home for the summer but I was able to convince them that I needed to stay at school. Not only was I rehearsing and playing gigs with *Haddonfield* at least once a week, but now that I had moved into an apartment my folks were going to be paying the monthly rent whether I was physically living in the place all summer long or not.

All that being said, I really just didn't want to go back to Baton Rouge.

I hadn't had much of a social life during my first year of college and my decision to move into a studio apartment off campus for my second year didn't do much to help my situation. High school had conditioned me to exist as a loner so my lack of friends during my first year of college didn't particularly bother me. I can freely admit that I didn't exactly make a lot of effort during my freshmen year, at least not after Howard dropped out of school.

When I had Howard it was a lot easier to walk into a party not knowing anyone yet as at least I had someone else to be a wallflower with me. After Howard had left school the mere thought of attending a social gathering gave me anxiety. I did still try a handful of times though. After all, just because I was accustomed to being alone it didn't mean that I *enjoyed* it. I was incredibly lonely but I also lacked the necessary confidence to walk into a party cold and strike up a conversation with complete strangers.

I'm sure it was just my own insecurity but I always felt as if every person at every college party already knew each other somehow. Even the very first night of freshman year, Howard and I had gone to an orientation party in the school's social center and from the second we walked in I got the feeling that everyone else there was already friends and I was an alien that had just landed on this earth from Mars. I couldn't fathom the way everyone at the party seemed to be laughing it up together as if they were old friends that had known each other for years. I mean, hadn't they all just arrived at college that same day, too?

What it really boiled down to was that the average person doesn't suffer from the same neuroses that my grade school experiences had imparted upon me. Howard was slightly more outgoing than I was so I'd basically follow him around each party and awkwardly stand beside him and nod whenever he would successfully strike up a conversation.

If the young woman Howard was speaking with also happened to have a friend acting as "wing woman" beside her, I would make an attempt at polite conversation with the friend. As luck would have it though, more often than not I was the odd man out in the social encounter and I would wind up just standing there and feeling like I was some kind of hovering creep.

It didn't help that there was always horrible dance music blaring at every party. Not only did I hate the music, I couldn't hear what anyone was saying even if an opportunity to talk to someone did arise.

Once Howard left school I still forced myself to go to a few more parties because I knew it was what I was supposed to do. I quickly developed my own process for attending social gatherings by myself and by my second solo outing I had my method down to a science.

I present to you…

Andrew Yong's 5-Steps to Attending Parties

Step 1: Enter the party and immediately begin walking around the perimeter as if you're looking for someone specific that you're supposed to meet up with there. This keeps you from standing in one place alone for too long and making it obvious that you have no friends. Be sure to keep a friendly smile on your face as you wander so that you come off like you're approachable and happy to be there. Occasionally change direction as if you've possibly spotted the person you're looking for or as if you've realized that you recognize someone else on the other side of the room.

Step 2: If you come across someone else who also appears to be at the party alone, try asking them a fundamental question that could potentially lead to a basic conversation. *"Do you know where the bathroom is?"* or *"Is that the line for the bar?"* are two examples of solid icebreakers. Both of those simple questions initiate basic human interaction without the social risk of putting yourself out there to be shot down. Hopefully, the person you ask for information is more outgoing than you are and will answer in a way that starts an actual conversation but if not, just say "thanks" and keep circling in search of your pretend friends.

Step 3: Once you've passed the same individual three times you'll need to momentarily take a break from your fake quest to find whoever it is that you're not really looking for. Stop wandering and get in the *longest* line you can find at the party. Whether it is the line for drinks, the line for the bathroom, or the line to request a song from the DJ… a long line gives you a solid reason to be seen standing around by yourself for several minutes and provides you with a break from fake circling. Once you've accomplished the purpose of whatever line you chose (for example- you've gotten a drink or you've stepped into the bathroom just long enough to make it seem like you've urinated), return to circling the perimeter. Note: Should you choose a bathroom line, under no circumstances should you remain inside the bathroom for more than ninety seconds or you'll risk making others think that you pooped while you were in there.

No one ever wants to talk to the guy at the party who just took a shit.

Step 4: For your final lap around the party you'll need to move just a little faster and with even more purpose in your step as others will more than likely have caught on to what you are doing by that point. Pray that during this final lap you actually *do* spot someone you've met before or that someone else at the party speaks to you.

Step 5: Leave.

I know that my method probably sounds lame but I assure you that pretending to look for friends that you don't actually have is far less lame than just standing around on display while not making any friends at all. If you try my process enough times eventually you'll get so good at it that you can be in and out of any party in ten minutes or less. After all, something is always on TV and it is not going to watch itself.

My batting average with friends and with women may have still been abysmal but one social aspect that I genuinely loved about UL Lafayette was that the school was way more diverse than my high school had been back in Baton Rouge. The campus was truly a melting pot of all different kinds of people and I no longer felt like I was the weird looking guy. Don't get me wrong, the student body was still about 65% white but there were way more non-white kids than where I had gone to high school. Most importantly, everyone seemed to get along. There were days during my freshman year where I would sit in the quad (the central courtyard between the classroom buildings) and just people watch. I remember thinking…*this is how it is supposed to be.* No one seemed segregated by the skin that they were born into. No one seemed to care about what anyone else looked like.

I couldn't have been more wrong as that was all about to change.

Over the summer heading into my sophomore year something would happen that would tear our country apart and bring the unspoken racial tension that had been bubbling just beneath the surface of our American society crashing into the forefront like a giant zit that had been burst across our country's shameful face.

On June 12th, 1994, two white people would be brutally killed on the other side of the country in the affluent neighborhood of Brentwood, CA. The only suspect in the double homicide was America's beloved football star, actor, and the guy from the Hertz rental car commercials… O.J. Simpson.

Simpson was an extremely successful black man who was a shining example of the American dream. The fact that he was now the only suspect in a gruesome double murder shocked the nation and his trial became an overnight obsession. When I first saw the news break on television I remember thinking "Oh shit, Nordberg from the *Naked Gun* movies killed some people. Crazy." I can honestly say that I didn't think much more about it and I felt that the country's fascination with the case was solely based on the fact that O.J. Simpson was a celebrity. As someone who had felt discriminated against for his entire life, I'm ashamed to say that I never saw the storm that was coming.

The United States of America began unraveling before my very eyes just five days later as the high profile celebrity case turned into a racially charged powder keg.

Only two years earlier Los Angeles had been all but burned to the ground in the historic LA riots which were the result of a group of white police officers being acquitted in the severe beating of a black man named Rodney King. While police violence was nothing new (especially with the LAPD who had a terrible reputation for letting cops get away with murder), the difference in the King case was that this time someone had actually caught it on video and there was undeniable proof. So when the officers who had committed the crime walked free… Los Angeles exploded with a rage that had been building up for decades causing over a billion dollars in damages, thousands of injuries, and over fifty deaths.

At first, it appeared that the prosecution had Simpson dead to rights with all of the seemingly undeniable evidence, but once Simpson's defense team of powerful lawyers brilliantly implied that the corrupt LAPD had planted all of the evidence, the Simpson trial became more about race and emotion and less about facts and logic. Given that Los Angeles had not even finished rebuilding from the Rodney King riots, society was still hurting and very much divided. By using the LAPD's horrible reputation as Simpson's defense, his attorneys silently threatened there would be more riots if the LAPD was to get away with this treatment of a black man again.

Once the Simpson trial began, the ripples of the defense team's racism theory would be felt across the country. Emotions ran incredibly high as the trial slowly made its way towards its conclusion.

Campus life at UL Lafayette would never be the same.

I was leaving class on Friday, June 17th when I noticed that there was no one in the quad. Usually the quad was filled with students talking, reading, studying, playing catch, or just enjoying the scenery between classes. Even in the summer when most students had gone home there was still always a crowd in the quad.

However, on this particular Friday evening, it was as if a zombie apocalypse had broken out while I was in class and every living person had vanished off of the earth. As I continued to walk towards my car I saw a massive crowd gathered in the Cypress Lake Dining Room, the campus' main restaurant. It was silent inside and everyone was facing the television.

As I slowly made my way into the restaurant my palms started to sweat with fear. Had another war broken out? Had there been a natural disaster somewhere in the world? The budding paramedic in me was scared that people were hurt and in danger somewhere and I was terrified of what was possibly on the television that could bring such a hush over a crowd of students that size.

On the screen was an aerial shot of a white Ford Bronco moving down a highway somewhere in Southern California. At least twenty police cars trailed behind the Bronco. I was too far away from the television screen to hear what was being said and I was too short to see over the heads in front of me so I couldn't read the graphics.

"What's going on?" I whispered to the guy directly in front of me.

He looked back at me and chuckled, "The Juice is loose."

Apparently, O.J. Simpson had failed to turn himself in to the authorities that morning and now he was in the back of the Bronco with a gun pointed at his own head. A close friend of Simpson's was driving the vehicle. You know the whole story. After all, 95 million people watched O.J.'s now famous "run for his life" take place live across every station in America. Chances are good that you watched it, too.

Before I even realized it, I had been standing there for an hour. I just couldn't pull myself away from what was happening and my eyes were transfixed on that white Bronco.

How was this going to end? Was Nordberg going to kill himself? Was the LAPD going to kill one of America's most beloved celebrities on live television? Was this really happening?

My legs and back were killing me from standing there for so long but my intense discomfort was secondary to my morbid fascination with seeing how this chase would end.

The Bronco pulled in to O.J.'s driveway and the police had him surrounded. Something huge was about to happen. I just didn't know *what.*

"Do you want to sit down?"

I turned around and saw the most beautiful woman I had ever seen in my life staring back at me. Like a scene from a movie, time briefly stood still and everything else in the room seemed to disappear.

She was a gorgeous young black woman with long black hair, giant round eyes, and flawless, almost glowing skin. I swear that somewhere in the restaurant someone had turned on a fan to blow her hair just slightly. Maybe it wasn't a fan that was causing her hair to flow. Perhaps it was my wildly beating heart that was creating the virtual breeze. The second we made eye contact it felt like someone had punched me in the chest and knocked the wind out of me.

I was in love.

Head over heels.

All of the power ballads I had spent years lip-synching in the mirror suddenly made complete sense to me in a crashing rush. It may sound like I'm exaggerating but I knew that I would marry her the moment I saw her.

And it would still be another hour before I even knew her name.

"Sure." I stammered back.

She motioned to the available space on the bench beside her and I sat down.

My life changed completely from that moment forward.

Sabrina Caruthers was and remains the strongest woman I've ever met. She had a magnetic force about her that most people couldn't resist. When she spoke, you listened. When she said she was going to do something, you never doubted her. When she looked at you, she saw right through you. She was incredibly intelligent and so well spoken that for the first few weeks that I was getting to know her I was completely intimidated.

All of that charisma, strength, intelligence, wit, passion, and ambition was wrapped up inside a woman that just so happened to look like a Greek goddess. She was physically perfect.

If Sabrina had wanted to be a supermodel she could have been one. If she had wanted to become an Oscar-winning actress she could have. An astronaut, a doctor, a soldier, the president of the United States…anything she wanted. You just knew that you were in the presence of success the second you got near her. Everyone was drawn to her and everyone that met her loved her.

If I wasn't the introverted and awkward guy that I was back then I probably would have proposed the very moment that I met her simply out of fear that someone else would leap in and marry her first.

When I look back at that night now, it is incredibly eerie for a number of reasons. There we were watching O.J. Simpson run from the police in what is now considered to be the bizarre opening ceremony to the "trial of the century," having no idea that thirteen years later

I would be the one standing accused of a murder at least twenty times as heinous in what the media would call the "trial of *this* century."

Like a classic Shakespearean drama, the lives of Sabrina and I were destined to become intertwined and then fall into great tragedy. However, in those first few moments nothing could have been more perfect.

The first thing I noticed about Sabrina was how wonderful I felt just being next to her. It was something that I never took for granted for the entire rest of our lives together. Just sitting next to her and holding her hand made me unbearably happy. We were never one of those couples that felt like if we weren't making continual conversation then something was wrong. Whether we talked for hours or sat next to each other in complete silence we felt just as close and content.

It was like that from the very first night we met.

As Sabrina and I watched the events at O.J.'s Rockingham estate unfold, our small talk turned from the crazy reality show playing out on the television to getting to know each other.

She was getting a degree in broadcasting. When I asked what exactly she hoped to do with that degree her answer said it all. *"I'm going to be bigger than Oprah."* There was not a shred of doubt in her voice and you could see in her eyes that she was absolutely going to achieve her dream.

Sabrina was from Queens, NY. I asked her why she hadn't gone to NYU or one of the many New York colleges that were much better known for their communications, film, television, and broadcasting programs.

"Because down here I have no competition," she said. "I'll be running things at this school within two years."

By the time we graduated three years later, I can assure you that Sabrina had been correct. She all but owned UL Lafayette's school of broadcasting with an unprecedented five shows on the school's network.

Yes, *five*.

Four of the shows were her own creations that she produced and directed on a weekly basis. But her main show ("The Sabrina Show") was a *daily* talk show, something else that had never been accomplished at UL Lafayette before Sabrina arrived.

The school had its own daily morning news program where the anchors rotated in and out in order to be fair to all of the students who wanted a crack at hosting on camera. As soon as it was explained to Sabrina that she could not be the *only* anchor on the school's daily news program, she went and created her own talk show.

By our junior year "The Sabrina Show" had become so big that she was pulling in real guests like Louisiana Governor Edwin Edwards and celebrity fitness personality Richard Simmons and not just notable students or professors from campus. Most of the students in the communications program worked for her. Hell, six of the school's professors even worked for her. It was a testament to her ambition and determination.

"The Sabrina Show" would go on to become a real television show right out of college. Sabrina never had to be an intern or an assistant. She never had to work her way up by starting in a mailroom, doing research, reporting, anchoring, or hosting for an already established show. She skipped right to having her own talk show on WDSU (an NBC affiliate based in New Orleans) when she was just 22 years old.

I need to point out that when "The Sabrina Show" began on WDSU Sabrina hired every single graduating student and professor that had ever worked for her for free during college. She created jobs and launched careers for all of them.

That was one of the greatest things about Sabrina. She may have been fiercely competitive and determined but in those early years, she never let her drive turn her into a cutthroat asshole that was only out for herself. If you helped her, she helped you.

How many college students have you ever met who took their professors with them when they graduated?

I'm sure that these days the board at UL Lafayette looks at Sabrina Caruthers as both the best and the worst thing to ever happen to their school. On one hand, she really put UL Lafayette on the map with her unprecedented success. On the other hand, she majorly screwed the school over when she took all but *one* of their broadcasting professors with her when she graduated.

Somehow this superhero of a woman who was perfect in every way fell in love with *me*. Sabrina could have had any man she wanted and yet she chose the quiet, introverted, Asian kid who had never even had a girlfriend before.

Yeah. I didn't get it either.

Once O.J. Simpson was carted away by the LAPD and the whole circus was over, the manager working at the Cypress Lake Dining Room announced that we'd all have to leave immediately. The restaurant had remained open almost three hours past closing time in order to accommodate the massive crowd that had gathered inside to watch the fiasco unfold across the country in Brentwood and the staff was anxious to close up and get home.

As I tried to find the courage to ask Sabrina for her phone number she surprised me by standing up and putting her hand out for me to take.

"Where to next?" She asked me.

I sheepishly told her that I wasn't sure. It was very late and I didn't really have any plans or know where I was going.

"That sounds perfect. Let's not know where we're going together," she said.

When I took Sabrina's hand it instantly felt familiar.

I had held her hand before in my dreams.

We spent the next six hours just sitting on the hood of my car and talking. The sun had come up around us by the time we said goodbye. We made plans to have dinner together two nights later, which was going to mean that I'd have to cancel band practice but I was fine with that.

I didn't tell Sabrina about *Haddonfield* or my secret double life as a wannabe rock star that first night. It's weird but every time I even considered mentioning it I felt foolish. Sabrina was so intimidating that the sheer thought of bringing up my band just seemed stupid. Once I mentioned I was the singer in a band she'd naturally ask if she could hear something and we hadn't recorded a single thing professionally yet. I'd wait and tell her about *Haddonfield* some other time when the moment was right.

Those next two days waiting to see Sabrina again were torture. I swear it felt like time was moving backward. I would wake up every 45 minutes, look at her phone number to remind myself that she wasn't just a dream and fall back into a restless sleep.

By the time the day of our date arrived I was more excited than I had ever been in my entire life. Having never dated before, I wasn't too sure of the protocol, but after two days of searching I had finally picked out an Italian restaurant that had solid reviews and seemed perfect. I called her that afternoon to let her know where I had made reservations and to ask what time she'd like for me to pick her up.

"You're sweet," she said, "but we're going to go to a sushi place on the other side of town and I'll pick *you* up at 6:45. See you soon!"

That was our relationship. Sabrina made all of the decisions and all of her decisions were final. I know that some men might not be okay with that but frankly, I loved it and it only made me even more enamored with her.

Sabrina chose the restaurant. Sabrina drove. And when the bill came at the end of the night, Sabrina insisted on paying. I may not have had any experience dating but I knew that in traditional dating the guy always pays for dinner so when our waitress walked by our table I whispered to her that it was Sabrina's birthday. A few moments later the wait staff came out singing "happy birthday" and put down a cupcake with a candle in it on the table. Sabrina was so confused and taken aback that I was able to grab the bill, throw in cash, and pass it off to our waitress before she could stop me.

It was a bold move pretending that it was Sabrina's birthday just so that I could pay for our meal, but I could see afterward that my quick thinking and determination had scored me major points.

When Sabrina dropped me off at the end of the night, she sternly told me that while she appreciated the gesture she didn't need a man to pay for her, even if it's a date. I told her that I already knew that she didn't need anyone to do *anything* for her and that's why I appreciated that she gave me the chance to buy her dinner.

She blushed. "Are you this smooth with all of the girls, Andrew Yong?"

"No. Just with you," I answered.

She gave me a quick kiss on the cheek. "I like you."

"I like you, too," I replied.

We said goodnight but before I got out of the car I asked when I could see her again. She started in on how busy she is during the week and said that she'd have to check and see if she was free the following weekend.

That wasn't soon enough for me.

Before I could think it through I blurted out, "I can't wait until next weekend to see you."

She laughed. "Well, maybe I can move something around."

"For tomorrow night?" I asked.

"Sure," she said and smiled huge.

Perhaps it was Sabrina's take-charge attitude that brought out the best in me, but whatever it was, I was a completely different person around her. Gone was the introverted, meek, and shy little boy that I once was. Her directness and blunt nature brought me out of my shell. Sabrina made me a far more confident person. Food tasted better. My classes were more interesting. I sang with more passion. Colors were brighter. My entire life was more…I don't know how else to put it, but… *alive*.

For our second date, we went to the movies and saw *Forrest Gump*. We held hands through the entire film and it was all I could focus on. I know the movie had something to do with shrimp and running but I could only focus on her hand in mine.

As I sat there in the darkness I remember thinking that every single thing in the world was now perfect. I never wanted *Forrest Gump* to end, even if I wasn't particularly paying attention to the movie.

I have to admit that I've still never actually watched *Forrest Gump* though I'm told it was quite the film. It even won six Oscars that year.

Our second date went so wonderfully that during the car ride home I felt confident enough to tell Sabrina about *Haddonfield.* I had never opened up about my lifelong dream to another human being so truthfully before that moment so in some ways it actually felt like a confession.

I wanted to tell her *everything*.

As I had feared, I hadn't even gotten to what kind of music we played before she asked if she could hear something. When I told her that we had not yet recorded anything she leaned over, turned off her radio, and simply said…"Sing."

Sing??? Here? In the car? A capella?

How embarrassing! I couldn't possibly…
But I did.

I sang to her.

With no fear.

I belted out a few lines to a *Haddonfield* song I had written called "Disenchanted."

"A picture book
In the hands of a child
Illiterate, an innocent smile
Unkempt and un-assured
Her eyes search the wind
Let her guard down
Pry her soul of sin..."

I wasn't very good. In fact, with my heart in my throat, I sang just about every note off key. Nevertheless I sang to her with no fear.

When I looked back at her she was crying.

"That bad?" I asked.

"No!" She replied. "That was the most romantic thing anyone has ever done on a date. Thank you. Thank you for sharing that with me."

Before I could speak… *she* began to sing.

Sabrina may as well have been a trained Broadway singer. She put me to absolute shame. I mean, of course she did. Anything I could do she could do better.

Hell, anything *anyone* could do Sabrina Caruthers could do better.

I know now that what she had sung to me were a few verses from "Music Of The Night", a song from Andrew Lloyd Weber's musical *Phantom of the Opera.* Sabrina loved show tunes and could sing every single one of them. She had taken voice lessons professionally and studied opera "just to see if she could do it."

That was Sabrina.

Now *I* was the one tearing up. What was happening to me? Just a few days earlier I had never been on a date in my life and now here I was, feeling happy and comfortable enough to be singing in the car with a beautiful girl I had just met!

I thought everything was going to be perfect for the rest of our wonderful lives together.

Chapter Three

The Love

Those first few months of dating Sabrina were magical but also very nerve-wracking for me. As exciting as it all was, in the very beginning I was always waiting for the other shoe to drop. I couldn't stop thinking that the dream cloud I was living on would suddenly disappear and leave me in a free fall back to the lonely reality I had always known. It was hard to fathom how I had gone from being virtually invisible to the opposite sex to dating a woman that most men would give everything they had just to be near.

Eventually, I came to understand why a girl like Sabrina would choose a guy like me.

In High School, the rules of attraction are pretty cut and dry where the beautiful, popular girls date the handsome, popular guys. If you weren't part of your high school's genetically elite, you needed to stick to your own dating league or just not date at all. I'd be lying if I said that college wasn't similar, however for someone as career-focused as Sabrina, she just wasn't interested in dating fraternity guys or football players. She knew what she wanted and that was someone who was not only stable and safe but also someone who would be happy playing the role of "supporting character" in the life she was hard at work creating for herself.

Sabrina needed a man that was content remaining behind the scenes and I fit that model perfectly. As serious as I was about playing with *Haddonfield*, I knew that the chances of me ever making it as a rock star were slim to none.

Sabrina never admitted it, but I know that deep down she never believed in my band either.

Even when I started making some money playing gigs on a regular basis, Sabrina still looked at *Haddonfield* as nothing more than a hobby of mine at best.

The first time Sabrina came to see us play we were the very first band performing on a five-band bill at a terrible dive bar. I had begged her to wait and come to another show when I knew there would be a bigger stage and a decent crowd but she was adamant that she didn't care how many people were there. She just wanted to see us play.

Including Sabrina, there were maybe seven people in the audience when *Haddonfield* went on. We had to play so early in the evening that the venue's sound engineer hadn't even shown up yet. The bartender merely flipped a switch that turned the PA system on and then told us to figure out the rest ourselves. We had no idea how the bar's archaic soundboard worked and no time to figure it out, so we went on without stage monitors to hear ourselves properly.

As if I hadn't already been nervous enough knowing that Sabrina was watching us for the very first time, I couldn't hear my own voice above the blaring guitar amplifier two feet behind me. The only sound more grating than my off-key singing was the constant feedback that would cause the people watching to cover their ears every few minutes.

To add insult to injury, we had to start the second song in our set over again after the drummer messed it up so badly that we couldn't figure out if we were in the verse or the chorus.

By the time our set came to an end, we had horrified everyone in the building. It was a complete disaster and the worst show we ever played.

Sure enough, the sound engineer conveniently showed up the very moment we unplugged our instruments.

Sabrina couldn't have been nicer about the travesty. She ran up to me afterward, beaming with pride and congratulating all of the other guys in the band on a great show. She even helped us carry our gear back outside to the drummer's van, impressing the other guys in the band as their girlfriends had never once helped out like that.

Though we had initially planned to stay and watch the other bands, we were all so defeated and embarrassed that we couldn't bear to set foot back inside the venue. We forfeited the $75 we were supposed to collect and just left.

Sabrina and I didn't speak a word to each other for the first ten minutes of the car ride home. She could see how upset I was and knew that I didn't want to talk about what had just happened.

That's when she said it.

"I love you, Andrew."

I said it right back as if I had already said those words a million times in my life.

"I love you too, Sabrina."

We slept together that night. Surprisingly, it wasn't as awkward as I assumed my first time would be. As with everything else in our relationship, Sabrina took charge and showed me the way.

Given how cutthroat of an entrepreneur Sabrina would eventually become, I can't help but wonder if things would have gone differently had *Haddonfield* performed well that night. Perhaps if Sabrina had gotten the impression that I stood a chance as a musician she would have been telling me goodbye instead of consummating our relationship.

Looking back I think that watching me bomb gave Sabrina confidence that I would never be in competition for her precious spotlight and that I would remain in the cheerleading section behind the scenes of <u>her</u> career.

I'd like to think that an Asian guy dating a black girl wouldn't have been such a big deal in the mid-nineties but given what the O.J. Simpson trial was doing to our country at the time, Sabrina and I would get nasty looks whenever we were out in public together.

The looks of contempt mainly came from black men.

Sabrina would always glare right back and challenge the disapproving person to actually say what they were thinking.

Of course, no one ever dared.

On October 3, 1995, the verdict was announced as to whether or not O.J. Simpson would be found guilty or innocent in the murders of Nicole Brown Simpson and Ronald Goldman. It was a tense day on campus and everyone was on edge waiting to see what would happen.

Sabrina and I had gathered in the quad with a few hundred other students to watch how the "trial of the century" would unfold. However, right before the verdict was about to be read Sabrina suddenly grabbed my arm and pulled me away from the crowd.

"What are you doing?" I asked her.

"Just in case," she said.

I was confused. How could we miss seeing the verdict?

"If he's guilty, there's going to be a riot and you're gonna get hurt," Sabrina said.

"But we all know he did it," I said.

"That's got nothing to do with this trial," she replied.

We were heading to the car to listen to the announcement on the radio when we heard the student body erupt in an even mixture of cheers and utter disgust. From the sounds emanating from the quad some three hundred yards away, we both knew the decision.

O.J. Simpson had been found innocent.

In the decades since the Simpson trial, there are jurors who have admitted that getting O.J. off was payback to the LAPD for Rodney King.

It's all so darkly poetic.

Sabrina and I got together during a crazy trial that captivated the world. Thirteen years later an equally sensationalized trial would break us apart.

******

I proposed to Sabrina the night after we graduated and we were married almost one year to the day later. Our wedding was relatively small since we both came from modestly sized families. While the wedding itself was average at best, our wedding *night* was anything but.

The moment we got to our hotel room Sabrina stripped off her wedding dress and stood before me, no longer as my beautiful girlfriend or fiancé but as my goddess of a wife. We didn't get out of bed until dinner time the next day. I could barely walk and there were several times during our 18-hour sex marathon where I was actually worried she might have to bring me to an emergency room.

I always thought that Sabrina and I had a pretty terrific sex life but our wedding night was something else completely.

Sadly, it was a closeness that I would never feel to her again.

I've heard comedians joke about how a wedding ring has a similar effect on women as the ring had on "Smeagol" in *Lord of the Rings*. That once a wedding ring slips onto a woman's finger she turns into "Gollum."

While I wouldn't necessarily compare Sabrina to "Gollum" (she certainly never let herself go physically and she was capable of being charming and sweet whenever she needed to be), within a month it became obvious to me that I was merely filling in the now checked off box of "husband" on her life's to-do list.

College degree? Check.

Insanely successful career lined up right out of school? Check.

Husband? Check.

Children?

… Children?

Hey, is this thing on?

Sabrina and I were on vacation in Hawaii for our first anniversary when she dropped it on me that she no longer wanted to have children. She said that her career was too important and she had no desire to ever become pregnant for fear of what the changes to her body might do to her precious TV show ratings.

I was shocked. Her revelation was so devastating to me that it felt as if we had somehow *lost* a child.

Ever the optimist, I assumed that she'd change her mind once her show had a stronger foundation and her career was more established.

Sadly, the more prominent and brighter Sabrina's spotlight became the less she was interested in even being a wife, let alone becoming a mother.

There were many nights where I felt more like a "thing" that had been collected in Sabrina's game of life and less like a partner or a lover.

We could only talk about *her* day and never mine. I was literally saving lives at work yet anything I had to share when I got home was insignificant to whoever Sabrina's guest had been that day or wherever her show had landed in the ratings.

Sabrina said that my stories were too upsetting for her and that she didn't like hearing about the various incidents I had responded to. It became evident over time that she just couldn't feign interest in anything other than herself.

I figured this is what the justice of the peace who married us meant when he said: "through better or for worse, through sickness and in health." Sabrina was working incredibly hard and as much as I had begun to resent her career, even I couldn't deny what she was up against in launching her very own television show.

Perhaps interviewing celebrities and hosting cooking segments wasn't quite as important as saving a child that had just been in a terrible car accident, but the difference was that I never had to worry about my career still being there the next day. The world is always going to need EMT's and I was damn good at my job.

In the entertainment business Sabrina was expendable and her show could suddenly fall apart without warning at any point, especially during those first few years.

So I chalked my frustrations at home up to career and marriage growing pains and I focused on being as supportive as I could be all while hoping for the cloud over our relationship to break.

In the meantime, I threw myself into my own career. It wasn't hard for me to do. I legitimately loved my job and the people I worked with. I hate to admit it but I was happiest when I was at work. It may sound crazy given the various disturbing tragedies I faced on a daily basis but when I was working I felt appreciated. I felt true camaraderie when I was among my fellow EMT's. I felt more love from the strangers I helped than I did at home.

For the next decade I was a husband to a woman that seemed to want to be anything but a wife.

Sabrina never wore her wedding rings in public, especially when she was on television.

"The male demographic of my audience doesn't want to think about me being married," Sabrina told me. "They want to think they have a chance at fucking me. It's just a fantasy, don't be offended."

But I was offended. Our wedding rings meant the world to me. If it weren't for our wedding photos, my co-workers likely never would have believed that I was married to the great *Sabrina Caruthers.*

Of course, she didn't take my last name when we got married. A black woman named "Sabrina Yong" would have only confused her audience.

I used to watch her show every day either before work or when I got home, depending on my shift.

Much to my surprise and delight, one day Sabrina actually mentioned me on her show. She was interviewing three firefighters who had become celebrities for fifteen minutes after saving twin infants from a house fire in New Orleans.

"My husband is an EMT and I know he takes his work home with him at night. How do the three of you shake off the trauma you witness every day?"

At that point, "The Sabrina Show" had been on the air for almost three years and it was the first time she acknowledged the fact that she was married. Sure, she didn't say my name but it was still a huge moment for me. It was the first time I ever got the sense that Sabrina knew and respected what I actually did every day.

When she got home that night I had bought her flowers and picked up sushi from her favorite restaurant.

"What's all this for?" Sabrina asked.

I kissed her long and hard.

"You mentioned me on your show today!" I said. "I just wanted to say thank you."

"Oh. That." She looked angry. "I slipped."

Ouch.

"You… slipped?"

"Andrew, I was speaking to three hot firemen and I got flustered. Hopefully, no one in the audience picked up on that. It could only hurt my image."

My heart shattered. "Yeah, let's hope no one heard that. God forbid anyone should know that I exist. I'd hate to hurt your image."

What she said next still hurts to this day.

"We've all made mistakes. I don't need the whole world to know about mine."

She might as well have pulled out a gun and shot me in the chest.

I didn't say anything back. How could I?

She went straight to bed without touching the sushi. The flowers stayed in the same spot on the table until they had rotted about a week later.

The next time I would watch my wife on television it would be seven years later from the comfort of a prison cell.

Chapter Four

The Argument

Fortunately our careers allowed Sabrina and I to stay in Louisiana. I never got the chance to know my own grandparents so I wanted to make sure that my children did. I was still very hopeful that once Sabrina was a bit more established in her career that she would come around to the idea of starting a family together. After all, plenty of TV stars had children.

I wanted the American dream of the perfect suburban home with the white picket fence. I could make a good living as an EMT and Sabrina was well on her way to making a very comfortable living as well. We certainly did well enough to support a family.

I never told my Mom that Sabrina had abruptly changed her mind about having kids. It would have broken her heart. The pitter-patter of little feet is something she longed for.

On September 13, 2006 my mother was diagnosed with pancreatic cancer.

She had been feeling sick for months and chose to ignore it. Pancreatic cancer is one of the most deadly forms of the disease, but with aggressive chemotherapy the doctors thought she stood a chance. I didn't know anything about what she was going through at first. My Mom kept it to herself. She didn't want it to affect our lives. That's the selfless person she was.

She probably would have held back on telling me about the cancer throughout the whole process if I hadn't seen her at the hospital.

We had just dropped off a young man that was found unresponsive after a drug overdose. There were moments in the ambulance when it seemed like we were going to lose him. One of the paramedics wanted to call it, but I refused. It's not always cut and dry when it comes to what we do. There are times when all seems lost, and then the heart begins to beat again. What if another twenty seconds of CPR or one more jolt from the paddles is all it takes to finally bring that patient back? The brink of death is steep but it is also long. Where everyone gets off is not the same. Ultimately I was able to save this man so I was riding a euphoric high as we handed him off to the emergency room staff.

As I walked down the hospital hallway I peered in a room absentmindedly. My mother sat in a chair, the IV in her arm delivering poison to her system, hoping to destroy the invading cancer. She was pale but otherwise looked like her normal self. I went into the room and asked her what she was doing there, but I already knew the answer. The question was asked more out of shock and denial.

I was scared but her resolve and demeanor made me believe that she'd be okay.

I felt guilty that I hadn't noticed earlier. The signs were there. She had lost some weight and her hair had begun to thin but I was too wrapped up in my own marital struggles to see it.

My father came in with flowers for her. He was always kind. She was his whole life. They never wavered in their love for each other. I'm sure they had their differences, all couples do, but they never stopped loving one another.

That's what I wanted with Sabrina.

"Don't worry about me," my Mom said. "I'm not going anywhere. I want to be around to meet my grandchild."

I didn't know what to say, so I lied and told my Mom that Sabrina and I were actively trying to make her a grandma. If you had seen the smile on her face, I swear it could have healed the world. My Mom had a way of doing that. She was so full of life and happiness. It radiated off of her like 'The Glow' in *The Last Dragon*.

From that day on, I went with my mother to her various appointments. I'd sit with her during the chemo and all she'd talk about was how great it was going to be to have a baby around again. I confided in her during one of the treatments that I was worried about being a good enough father.

"And you should be," she said to me. "Bringing a life into the world is the easy part. The hard part is taking that life and guiding it, teaching it right from wrong."

"How did you know how to do it?" I asked.

A wave of nausea hit my Mom at that moment. She closed her eyes and breathed through her nose, slowly and methodically. I held her hand until it passed. She opened her eyes after a moment and looked deeply into mine.

"I didn't," she smiled. "I learned how to be your mother simply by loving you. That's the most important thing. Love that child with everything you've got and never give up on it."

My Mom passed away six days later.

At the funeral Sabrina held my hand and consoled me at the appropriate times, but it felt hollow; like she was going through the motions.

When we got home we barely exchanged a word. Sabrina may have volunteered to organize the funeral arrangements for my Dad and I, but emotionally it felt like my actual pain was nothing more than a burden on her. I was going to have to go through my grieving process alone.

I had been battling depression and having trouble sleeping in the weeks leading up to my mother's passing. My doctor had prescribed an anti-anxiety pill to help me cope but the truth is that the pills didn't do anything for my actual heartbreak. They merely made me groggy enough to sleep with my heart in pieces.

I had watched my mother slowly and painfully wither away and die before my eyes.

Now I was watching my marriage go through the same slow and agonizing death. Feeling so disconnected from my wife, I thought my pain couldn't possibly get any worse.

I was wrong.

Though Sabrina went back to work as usual the next day, I exercised my option of taking three bereavement days. Wanting to keep myself busy I went to work sorting through almost two weeks of mail that had piled up on the kitchen table.

I came across something that stopped me in my tracks.

It was a piece of mail from a clinic I recognized.

The letter was addressed to Sabrina but fearing the worst I couldn't wait for her to get home. I opened the letter and began reading it.

She was pregnant.

Was.

She apparently had the abortion the day before my Mom passed away.

All the wind fell out of me and I collapsed to the floor. I couldn't believe she would make such a huge decision without even telling me.

I sat on the floor for hours. I was still there when she came home. She looked at me and then saw the clinic paperwork in my hand.

I thought she would cry and feel bad about terminating our child.

She didn't.

I thought she'd feel guilty about not telling me.

She didn't.

"What gives you the right to open my mail?" She snatched the paper out of my hands.

"How could you do this?" I asked.

"It's my body, Andrew," she replied.

"I understand that but don't you think you could have at least *discussed* it with me first?" I asked.

"There was nothing to discuss. I told you that I don't want children. It was a fucking accident."

"You couldn't even tell me!" I shouted.

"You were already having a hard enough time with your Mom dying. I didn't want to overwhelm you."

"That's bullshit, Sabrina," I replied, standing up angrily.

"Well, at least we can stop pretending. I hated lying to your mother and acting like we were trying to have kids."

I had never felt so angry before. I was going to explode. I did the only thing I could think of.

I left.

There was no denying that our arguments were getting worse and worse. I didn't want either of us to say something we couldn't come back from and the couch was too close for comfort. So I walked out. I didn't have a plan or know where I was going. I just left and started driving around hoping to center myself. Before I knew it I was downtown in the Quarter.

The French Quarter is the premier tourist stop in the New Orleans area. The decadence and debauchery of Bourbon Street is what we are most known for. These days Victor Crowley is a close second. Like most communities, the locals tend to avoid the touristy area and all of the traps it provides. Sure, we like the money that the constant tourism brings in, but we don't always like the tourists themselves.

I knew that I could disappear into my own head in the Quarter. Large crowds, especially those that are inebriated, tend to not notice what is going on around them. They are attracted to the pomp and circumstance. I would be left completely alone in the mosh pit of humanity swirling down those busy streets.

I'm not much of a drinker so drowning my sorrows in booze wasn't an option. I always try to turn a negative into a positive and you can't do that when you have a clouded mind. I looked at everyone passing me by. They seemed happy. Grins were plastered on their faces as they goofed off enjoying New Orleans' splendor. I wanted to be happy, too. I didn't understand why I couldn't be.

Sabrina and I had achieved almost every goal we set out to accomplish. On paper, our lives were damn near perfect but once you left the page the trouble started.

I bought a yellow notebook.

I was going to craft a song for her. Through writing songs I'm able to share my soul in a way that I otherwise couldn't. Of course that could just be the wannabe rock star in me.

I needed a place to hole up for a night or two, cool down, and write. My writing process is very introverted. I know some writers like to go to a coffee shop to create. They usually say it's about being around other people. Life around them spawns life on their laptop.

I think that's bullshit.

Most just want to be seen writing. It makes them feel important.

I knew I couldn't go back home for a bit. It was too volatile there. Being that it was Mardi Gras I also knew this was the worst possible time to try to find a hotel room. Prices would be jacked up and there was little chance that I would find a vacancy.

I was walking down St. Peter Street when two young guys stopped me.

One was a tall lanky fellow wearing a T-shirt with a weird smiley face on it. The other was a black man wearing dozens of strands of cheap plastic beads around his neck; the true sign of a tourist in the Big Easy.

"Excuse me, buddy," the lanky one said. "We're looking for the voodoo shop that does the haunted swamp tours. Can you help us out?"

"No, sorry," I answered honestly. I shrugged them off and quickly walked away.

In a strange twist of fate both young men would wind up being among the victims that weekend. I recognized the smiley face T-shirt immediately the first time I saw photos of the missing and the dead published on the evening news.

I had done a swamp tour once when I was in college just to see what it was all about. I wound up bored with over fifty chigger bites. Perhaps if I had taken just a moment to warn them what a waste of money the swamp tours are they would have done something else that night and still been alive.

But how could I have ever known?

A "vacancy" sign in a window ahead captured my attention. The Hotel Katharine. At least that's what it was called ten years ago.

Katharine is a name I've always loved. My favorite movie of all time is *On Golden Pond* and of course Katharine Hepburn shines in that role. I'm a firm believer in the universe giving us signs. So when I saw that the hotel name was spelled exactly the same as the actress, I knew that was going to be my spot to ride out the emotional car crash I was in the midst of.

I didn't have anything with me other than the notebook I had picked up but that was all I needed.

I checked into the room and collapsed on the bed. The emotional exhaustion of the week finally caught up with me. I cried for an hour straight and then slept for almost another ten hours.

I spent most of my second night there pouring my heart out on the pages of the notebook and then crumpling them up and throwing them away. It took a few hours but eventually I found my path into the song. It came on in a sudden surge and I felt like I finally tapped into my soul.

I was pleased with what I had created for Sabrina. I thought the song could serve as a solid olive branch in helping her and I begin to get back on the right track. I labored over every word to make sure the lyrics were exactly right. And they were. I still think they are. I called it "IN THE DARK (Sabrina's Song)".

I woke up the next morning feeling refreshed and content. I felt a tinge of positivity flowing through me for the first time in months. I had weathered the passing storm over the last two nights and it was a new day filled with possibilities.

I wanted to call her and sing her the song. I imagined it bringing her to tears. Good tears. I would hear the love in her voice and the passion that I knew was still in her heart.

I picked up my phone to call and I immediately became nervous. It felt like calling up a girl and asking her on a date for the first time. That's what we had to do back in our day. There was no swiping right, no emails, no texts. You had to be brazen enough to make actual verbal contact. It was always something I was terrible at. I'd clam up, I'd sweat, and my stomach would get queasy. It was a horrible feeling as for me asking a girl out had always led to rejection. But you never knew the outcome unless you tried.

How had it become so hard to share feelings with my own wife? Someone I felt a deep connection to? Someone I was in love with and spent every day of my life with for years?

I began to dial Sabrina's cell phone number and then hung up. My hands were shaking. I needed to steady myself. I decided to eat first. Food sometimes helps calm the jitters.

I was sitting in the lobby of the hotel eating a bagel and reading the handwritten lyrics I had composed when my phone rang. I picked it up off of the table quickly, expecting it to be Sabrina. She had to be worried and wonder where I had been. I had been gone two days and I never told her I was staying in a hotel.

Unfortunately, it wasn't Sabrina on the other end of the phone.

If only I hadn't answered.

Chapter Five

The Legend

Once upon a time, there was a boy named Victor Crowley. He was born with a rare congenital disorder known as Wiedemann syndrome that left him horribly disfigured. According to Louisiana lore, Victor's father Thomas Crowley had been having an affair with his dying wife Shyann's nurse, a young Cajun woman named Lena. In Shyann's final breath she put a voodoo curse on Thomas and Lena's unborn child.

On the day that Victor Crowley was born, they say that the swamp wept. The bayou became temporarily toxic and nearby wildlife became sick and died. Lena herself would pass away while giving birth to Victor.

In the years that followed, Thomas kept Victor hidden away in his house out in Honey Island Swamp. Some say Thomas was trying to protect Victor from the eyes of a cruel and unaccepting world, but others believe he was merely trying to hide his own shame and infidelity. Regardless, it was only a matter of time before enough people caught a glimpse of young Victor and the locals began to whisper about "the monster" that Thomas Crowley was keeping secret out in the swamp.

Many years later on Halloween night, three local children paid a visit to the Crowley house while Thomas was out. They threw firecrackers at the front porch and tried to scare Victor, now a grown man, outside so that they could see "the monster" for themselves. It was an accident, but the front of the house caught fire and Victor was trapped inside.

Thomas arrived home in time to see the three masked children flee the scene. In an effort to try and save Victor from the fire, he grabbed a hatchet and began frantically chopping down the front door. Unbeknownst to Thomas however, Victor was pressed up against the other side of the door trying to escape from the fire. Thomas accidentally hit his son in the face with the hatchet… and poor Victor Crowley died.

Thomas was convinced that he knew the children responsible for the tragedy. He reported them to the police but the kids and their parents denied everything and no one was ever arrested or held accountable. Thomas Crowley would spend the last few years of his life as a recluse and eventually die of a broken heart.

That's when the terrifying rumors began to circulate through the area.

Supposedly Victor Crowley returned to Honey Island Swamp after Thomas passed away. Night after night his vengeful spirit would roam the bayou, crying out in search of his father, the only love he ever knew. Local hunters and fisherman began to disappear only to turn up in pieces. Over the years enough bodies had piled up that the authorities had no choice but to shut down Honey Island Swamp and condemn the public from the area.

According to folklore experts and scientists in the field of paranormal studies, Victor Crowley is what's known as a "repeating poltergeist," meaning that his manifestation is cursed to return every night in the same physical state that he originally died in.

But that's not the scariest part.

For whether you believe in ghosts or not, as legend has proven again and again over the last several decades, once you've heard Victor Crowley crying for his Daddy... it's too late.

You're already dead.

- Louisiana Folklore

Chapter Six

The Day

My boss, Jim Duffy, was on the other end of the phone. Jim had hired and mentored me. He wasn't the type to mix work with pleasure unless we were talking about snacks. The man loved to eat treats and I had always privately thought that would end up being the death of him.

I would wind up being wrong about that.

Given that I was still on bereavement leave, I immediately knew something big was going on if Jim was calling me. With it being Mardi Gras, there was already a full staff scheduled each day. More than enough EMT's to handle the usual shenanigans in the French Quarter during this time of celebration. Jim calling meant that something significant had gone down.

It was something I could never have imagined in my wildest nightmares.

"Hello Jim," I said, answering the phone while trying to swallow the bite of jalapeno and cheese bagel in my mouth.

"I'm sorry to bother you right now, bud, but I'm going to need you to come in," he said, getting right to the point in his unmistakable gruff tone. "Now."

"What happened?" I asked, expecting the worst.

"It's a total shit show," he said. "Just get to the station as soon as you can."

The station is like most. There are large bay doors for the vans and ambulances. We have a few sleeping quarters similar to a fire department. That way someone is always there ready to respond in the blink of an eye. A moment's delay can be the difference between living and dying.

We have a nice kitchen that always retains the smell of Cajun spices, even when we try to avoid that. Creole cooking is fantastic, there's a reason so many travel to New Orleans for its authenticity. I think it's one of the best cuisines in the world.

My family may have been Chinese but my mother made some of the best Cajun food I ever had. She called it "Casian" food.

Get it?

Yong Family Casian Seasoning

4 teaspoons Cayenne Pepper
5 tablespoons Paprika
2 tablespoons Onion Powder
2 tablespoons Garlic Powder
2 tablespoons Dried Oregano
1 tablespoon Dried Thyme
2 tablespoons Dried Basil
2 tablespoons Black Pepper
5 tablespoons Seasoning Salt

Mix all the ingredients together and store it in a sealed container in the refrigerator. You will not find a better seasoning in a supermarket.

When I arrived at work Jim was on the phone in his office. I peered in and he waved me off. Whoever was on the line was important. I had listened to the news on the way over and heard nothing. There was no major catastrophe to speak of. I had no idea what was going on.

While I was waiting I realized that I didn't have my work clothes on. Protocol states that I had to be in uniform, it cuts through the constant explaining you'd have to do on the scene without it. You'd think a crime scene would be sacred but all sorts of people try to sneak in for a look. It's human nature. Rubbernecking is a real thing and has been a thorn in the side of many highway travelers.

Luckily for me I kept a spare uniform in my locker. I was getting dressed when Randy walked in.

Randy Gibson is the person I was closest to on the team. We were good friends in addition to coworkers. He had a fun sense of humor, something you need on this job to take you away from what you are dealing with, even if it's just a short respite. He loved to put peanut butter in his mouth and pretend he was the guy from the "Got Milk?" commercial trying to say "Aaron Burr."

He was a horror movie fan. He had an almost encyclopedia level knowledge of the genre. The fact that he went into the line of work he did was practically stereotypical. Personally, I never understood horror. Why would someone want to be scared? I don't find it entertaining and thought those that did probably had something wrong with them.

Randy was a sweet soul though. He always had a smile and was kind. So kind. He taught me quite a bit about not judging a book by its cover. He once showed me a movie called "*Night of the Living Dead*". I would never have watched it, but during a poker game at the station, we had all agreed that the winner could pick the movie. Cards and TV tended to be our break from boredom during a slow, overnight shift. Randy won and we honored the bet. While it didn't change my mind about horror films, I did find the subtext and the craft that was woven through the story to be quite intelligent and thought-provoking. It was the perfect analogy for Randy.

"Good morning sunshine," Randy said, as he walked over to me.

"You get called in too," I replied, knowing he was also scheduled off today.

"Nah, I just missed you. I couldn't go another day without seeing your face."

I laughed. Randy always had a way of making me laugh.

Laughter is such a beautiful thing. It can genuinely heal and connect us, even if it's only for a brief moment. I miss laughing. I haven't been able to for quite some time.

"What did you do last night?" Randy asked.

I didn't know how to answer. I wasn't going to tell him the truth. I kept my personal life well-guarded. I could have just muttered a "not much". But the question brought me right back to the thoughts and feelings I had temporarily forgotten about. I felt like I stared at him for hours without answering. It was probably only a few seconds but fortunately for me, we heard the door open and turned towards it.

Bob came walking in. He was a decent guy, good to have around because he worked hard and was always ready to lend a hand. He was the strongest of us. If Bob got called, that meant that we needed strength.

"I don't want to interrupt your circle jerk, but do either of you know why we are here?" Bob asked.

"No idea," Randy said.

Bob looked into Jim's office.

"Have either of you talked to Jim?" Bob asked.

"Nope. I just got here," Randy answered.

Bob turned his attention to me.

"What about you Yong?" He asked.

"No. He's been on the phone since I got here," I replied, finally able to break my silence.

"I see," Bob said, "well I'll find out."

Bob walked into the office. Jim covered the mouthpiece of the phone as they exchanged a few brief words. After a few seconds, Bob nodded and disappeared into a closet behind Jim's desk. He came out dragging a box.

"Help me with this," Bob said as he exited the office. "We have to load it in the van."

I bent down, grabbed an end of the box and helped him carry it to the van.

"Did he tell you what's going on?" I asked him.

"No, but it must be bad if he's having me dig this out," Bob replied.

"What is this?" I asked as we set the box down. I didn't recognize it.

"This," he said as he flipped the top of the box open revealing its contents, "means a long fucking day."

I looked into the box.

It was full of body bags. A significant amount more than I had ever seen at once. I would later learn that the nickname for it was "Katrina stock".

In the event that a massive disaster occurred these could be used.

"Are we ready gentlemen?" Jim asked as he walked up behind us.

"Yes sir," Bob replied.

"Good. Let's go then," Jim said, as he crawled into the van. "Bob you can drive."

The guys never let me drive. They had made a stupid game out of never even letting me touch the keys. It was part of their on-going joke about me not being a good driver simply because I'm Asian. I would have taken offense but I did actually crash the van once.

For the record, it wasn't my fault.

"Aye Aye captain," Bob said, as he crawled into the driver's seat. "Where are we heading?'

"Honey Island Swamp," Jim said.

I looked at Randy and we exchanged a knowing glance.

"Honey Island Swamp? No one goes out there," I quietly said to Randy.

"*Somebody* did," he replied before glancing down at the box of body bags. "A whole lot of somebodies."

The dock was a short drive away. We loaded everything on the ambulance boat and we were off and running.

As our boat made our way out into the bayou I looked around. There is a calm beauty to the swamp during the daytime but I certainly did not want to be out there at night.

Honey Island Swamp had been closed for many years. It was illegal to even go there. Officially they said it had to do with excess methane. Too much swamp gas was poisonous. It made much more sense than the legend.

I knew the legend.

We all did.

I inquired about whether we should be wearing a gas mask for protection and Jim just smirked and shook his head.

The first thing I noticed as we entered the swamp was the sound, or more to the point, lack of sound. It was quiet other than the insects.

It was eerie.

They say silence can be maddening and this was my first taste of what that truly meant.

I looked at Randy and he was grinning like a kid in a candy store. Of course he was. It was creepy. It was totally in his wheelhouse.

"Have you ever been called out here?" I asked, more to break the silence than anything.

"No," he replied looking around. "I've always wanted to see it though. What about you?"

"Hell no," I replied. "I've heard all the stories."

"That's the main reason I've always wanted to visit. It's like a horror movie come to life," he said. "Can't you feel it? Something feels off here. It's awesome."

I didn't quite share his sentiments. I wanted to get out of there as soon as I could. He was right, it felt off. But we had a job to do.

"We may be entering the Dagobah system," Randy said as he held a flashlight up like a saber.

I smiled. I got that reference. While I am not a horror fan I do love my sci-fi and *Star Wars* especially always makes me grin. It takes me back to being a kid. The grin fell away quickly though as we could finally see some life ahead.

It was time to get down to business.

We arrived late to the party. There were already many people there working on the scene. We docked on the shore and began to prepare.

"What do we need?" I asked Jim.

"Everything," he replied, as he walked off of the boat.

I looked where he was heading and sighed. Deputy Hamilton was moving towards the boat.

I hated Hamilton.

Then again, everyone hated Hamilton.

How he became a deputy I'll never know. He only had one eye. Certainly, I did not look down upon him for that. We are all dealt hardships we have to overcome and he obviously overcame his since you have to have excellent vision in order to become a sheriff deputy that works in the field.

As a medical professional, I know his depth perception would be far less than would be required in order to carry a weapon. Word was that he had an older brother on the force that pulled a lot of strings to get him the job.

What I do know is we all hated him. He was the quintessential douchebag. Without the badge, he was an arrogant prick. With the badge as a shield, he was even worse. He was a bully and liked to talk shit and bark orders like he ruled the world.

He would no doubt make our job more difficult. Jim had somehow avoided meeting Hamilton prior to this call. I'm not sure how.

He had been lucky.

Jim and Hamilton began to converse. I moved near them in order to get as much info as I possibly could.

I had never seen so many people working a scene. At least five other Parish's had provided their EMT's.

"How many bodies are we talking about here?" Jim asked. "Three? Six?" He added sarcastically.

"Thirty or more," Hamilton replied.

"What happened?" Jim asked.

"Jefferson Parish PD has a girl in custody," Hamilton assured him.

I remember that clearly. He was so confident that they knew who did this. Almost like it was an open and shut case.

I looked over in time to see a first responder walk past carrying the top half of a severed head.

A *girl* in custody?

One look at the scale of the crime scene and anyone with any sense at all knew there was no way a lone woman could have done all this. Frankly, no man could have possibly done all of this either.

But we aren't talking about a man.

We're talking about Victor Crowley.

I was one of the EMT's that bagged his body.

At the time I had no way of knowing that it was indeed him but just looking at the body gave me chills. He was massive and his skin was covered in all kinds of muscular deformities. There was no head to speak of. It was just hunks of flesh and tissue hanging in its place. He wore an old pair of overalls and big black boots. Exactly how tall he was is tough to say due to the condition we found his body in. He had been crudely cut in half, bisected right down the middle and lying on top of the biggest chainsaw I had ever seen. Bob, who helped me bag the body, called it a "Redwood chainsaw". All I know is that it was about six feet long.

The chainsaw was evidence so we waited for the officers to remove it before bagging the body. Our job was to remove corpses and not touch *anything* else unless specifically instructed to do so and only after it had been photographed and tagged.

It took three officers to carry the chainsaw away. I remember thinking that there was no way someone could wield it by themselves.

Bob and I exchanged a knowing glance as we began to bag the body. Neither of us said the words, but we both had an eerie feeling about *who* exactly we were handling.

He was real; *he was actually real…* and also quite dead. Nevertheless, I was still scared of him. But I pushed the fear away and focused on the task at hand.

We struggled to carry the body to the boat. We had to set him down a few times. It was during one of these breaks that one of the volunteer "reserve" EMT's approached us carrying something large and metallic in his hands. It was a guy I've only ever known as "what's-his-name."

Let me explain.

Every Parish in Louisiana had a handful of volunteer "reserve" EMT's that worked with the team when needed but who were not actually *part* of the team. After the disaster of Hurricane Katrina, a lot of volunteers had come out of the woodwork hoping to help make a difference. These were not career first responders but eager individuals who had taken weekend certification courses in the basics like CPR training.

Don't get me wrong, on big jobs like this the volunteer "reserve" EMT's were very much appreciated but they were merely an extra set of hands looking to earn some extra cash when they could pick up the work. Of course with a day such as this, where the job at hand is so massive that every Parish within a five-hour drive has been called in, the volunteer "reserve" EMT's would be out in force.

I'm sure you've been in similar situations in your own careers and social lives but there comes a point where you've met an individual enough times that you should really know his or her name. After that point, it would be incredibly awkward and make you look like an asshole if you were to ask. I had worked with "what's-his-name" on and off for almost two years at this point and the time period for asking him to tell me his name had long since expired.

Thus the name "what's-his-name."

On the off chance that I had to work with "what's-his-name" I would get around saying his name by using the tried and true method of just referring to him as "buddy," "dude," or "man" when having to address him directly. It didn't help that I had always found "what's-his-name" to be a pretty lazy and sloppy worker who was clearly just there to pick up some extra income. In my defense, I think that's why I just never bothered to learn his name.

"What's-his-name" never seemed to be able to follow even the simplest of directions. Whether it was putting items back in their correct place or merely coiling a cable the correct way, he was always more of a hindrance than any kind of real help.

Case and point; the belt-sander he was carrying over to us in his hands. More accurately, a *gas-powered* belt-sander.

I didn't even know something like that existed until that moment.

"Hey, since you guys are going back to the boat can you take this with you?" "What's-his-name" asked.

He set the heavy sander down on top of our giant bag, adding even more weight to the enormous body we were already barely managing to carry.

"Thanks," he said before wandering off into the brush in the same direction he had just come from. Most likely to try and hide out and not actually help until specifically given a task to do by a superior officer at the scene.

It was classic "what's-his-name" behavior.

"Is that sander gas powered?" I asked Bob, bending down and grabbing my side of the body bag again.

"Looks that way," Bob said as he picked up his side. "Now come on. We've got weather coming in."

Almost on cue, the clouds rolled in and it began to sprinkle. We rushed to the boat as fast as we could.

Bob and I set the body and the sander down together on the deck. Randy noticed the size of the bag we were carrying and came over to see what we had.

"What did you guys bring me, a giant?" He asked, intrigued.

"Yeah, it's hard to tell. He was lying on a chainsaw and his body was in pieces. We haven't found the majority of his head yet." I replied. "I think you may want to look at this one right away. He has all sorts of muscle and skin deformities… and he's wearing overalls."

"Get the fuck out," he said, as the wheels began spinning in his head.

"I think he may be a crucial component in all of this," I replied.

"You don't think it could be…" Randy asked, his demeanor noticeably changing to an almost morbid excitement.

"All I'm saying is you might want to drop whatever you're doing and make this the priority," I said, cutting him off.

"Awesome. I mean, creepy… but awesome," Randy replied, as we carried him inside.

I left the belt sander out on the deck.

It was a mistake that would come back to haunt me later in the night.

The ambulance boat itself had a much larger work area than I expected. From the outside, it seemed to be tiny, but once inside it was remarkable just how well designed and efficient it actually was.

Ambulance swamp boats aren't a prevalent thing. I don't know the history of them but I wouldn't be surprised if they were created specifically for Honey Island Swamp given the number of times search and recovery teams in that jurisdiction had been out there over the years.

I'm not saying that as Louisiana EMT's we didn't respond to our fair share of emergencies in other bayous where getting a vehicle out there just wouldn't be possible, but from everything I had ever heard Honey Island Swamp had always been synonymous with trouble.

Let's just say that in all of my years as an EMT I never once heard of a team called to Honey Island Swamp for a treatable emergency and not just a collection of carcasses.

Of course the first time I had to go out there it was the worst situation in the swamp's already sordid history.

Randy and I put the body on the cold slab. He genuinely seemed to be fascinated by the situation. Not that I was surprised given his macabre infatuation with horror movies and the occult.

The bad feeling that set root when we had first arrived was now raging inside my chest tenfold. There was something incredibly wrong here. I was on edge and this led to a conversation that I have thought about endlessly ever since.

"Crazy shit," Randy said, "I was just working on an Asian male that has his head cut off and his leg missing below the knee. He actually looks like *you*."

The racial joking was nothing new, especially coming from Randy who seemed to live for busting my balls. Usually I wouldn't have gotten offended but I was in Honey Island Swamp looking at the body of what I was sure had to be Victor Crowley and night was quickly approaching. I just wanted to finish up and get the hell home so I let my emotions get the best of me and took it out on the wrong person.

"Oh, 'cause us Asian's all look the same, right?" I snapped back, angrily.

"Just kidding man," Randy said, holding his hands up.

"Asshole," I replied, storming away.

I'll always regret that.
Randy was my friend and a good guy.

I never saw him alive again.

Chapter Seven

The Night

If you are squeamish or have a weak stomach I suggest you bypass this chapter. The graphic details contained on these pages will likely give you nightmares similar to the night terrors I've had to live with ever since that horrible night. Even a decade later every time I close my eyes I still see, hear, and smell the hell that I lived through in that swamp. I've undergone years of counseling, various forms of therapy, and countless medications for my post-traumatic stress but it has never gotten any easier. I'm hoping that by sharing all of this it will help take away some of the power the tragedy still holds over me.

Also if you are skipping directly to this chapter you are missing the entire point of this book. I implore you to go back and read from the beginning. This book is about my life. I am more than just the gruesome events of a single night.

The sun had set and darkness engulfed the swamp. It was a full moon that weekend which created an ominous glow all around us. Now that night had fallen the non-stop insect serenade only grew even louder.

Every time I thought we had the all clear to go home another victim (or piece of a victim) would be discovered.

Time was of the essence as the longer the bodies remained in the swamp the faster the wildlife and other elements would swallow them up. With every passing minute, the remains of what had once been someone's child, parent, husband, wife, or other loved one was being consumed by the bayou's gators, birds, rats, and hordes of hungry mosquitoes. The higher-ups in charge weren't about to call off our search and recovery for the night just because of a ghost story that had most of us uneasy about staying in Honey Island Swamp after dusk.

There was no bathroom out there so we had to find our own little private places to relieve ourselves. I was standing against a tree doing just that when I heard a voice call out from behind me.

"Freeze!"

Police officers from several counties had been in the swamp with us all day and I had become accustomed to their voices. This one was different though. There was power behind it. He didn't sound like one of the locals. There had been rumors swirling around that a Special Forces team was coming in. Par for the course as you can't have a body count as large as the one we were dealing with without the big guns swooping down to take over.

"Put your hands up and turn around slowly," the voice called out.

I put one of my hands up but the other was still holding my business.

"Put your other hand up, NOW!" He barked with even more heft.

"I can't," I replied nervously.

"I'll give you to the count of five and then I'm going to put a round in the back of your head!"

He was threatening to shoot me? I was beyond confused.

"One!"

I tried to will my flow to stop but my fear only made it increase.

"Sir, I'm with the recovery team," I said.

"Two!"

I didn't want to turn around and urinate all over the officer but I couldn't stop.

"Three!"

"Sir please, I can't turn around right now!" I begged.

I began to feel the flow subsiding.

"Four!"

I pushed with all my might, trying to empty my bladder. I heard a click behind me.

The stream stopped. I quickly put things away and zipped up.

"Five!"

I spun around with my hands up.

Hamilton, that eyepatch-wearing son of a bitch stood before me grinning. He put his gun away and I relaxed for a moment. I was no longer in fear for my life. Instead, I was seething with anger. There was so much devastation and death surrounding us. This was not the time to joke around. Truthfully, shooting someone should never be a joke.

"Bad taste," I said trying not to sound scared or angry. Having dealt with bullies my whole life I knew that either emotion was likely to only encourage him to keep going.

"Bad taste?" He said with a smirk on his face. "You're the one pissing on my crime scene."

I looked around. The area I was in was devoid of any signs of the massacre. "Where should I have gone?"

"Piss in the swamp," he said.

I knew better than to put myself in a position like that. We were in the bayou after all. A gator could leap up and bite my junk off for all I knew. I tried to think of something to say back but before I could Hamilton walked away laughing.

I hate speaking ill of the dead but I really fucking hated him.

I walked away muttering obscenities under my breath and bumped into a deputy that I didn't know. I've since been able to identify him as Mendoza. Our interaction was short, but in it I found kindness.

"Don't mind him none," he said, "that guys a fuck head."

"Thank you," I said, relieved to find that someone in his ranks agreed with my opinion of Hamilton.

"What's the good word?" I asked, hoping to get some news in regards to our departure.

"I think we are going to head out soon," he replied.

"Thank God," I said.

"Ain't that the truth," he replied as he patted me on the shoulder and walked away.

I began heading back in the direction of the boat.

"Hold up," Mendoza yelled.

I turned around to see he was on his radio.

"Scratch that. They just found a whole different group of victims," he said. "Come on, this way."

Gunshots suddenly rang out back in the direction of the boats.

It had to have been at least ten shots fired and they sounded like they all came from the same weapon in rapid succession.

Mendoza and I froze. He began calling on the radio asking for information. A garbled response came back as radios all over the swamp started checking in at once. Finally, a reply came back for us both to stay put as there was a group of officers headed our way.

I could tell that Mendoza was just as okay with that order as I was. If there was a reason for an officer to discharge ten or more rounds of his weapon I didn't want to go blindly racing into whatever was going down until I knew the trouble had passed and the coast was clear.

We made small talk as the minutes passed.

"You don't think Hamilton actually shot someone trying to be funny, do you?" I asked.

"Hamilton's a dick but he's harmless," Mendoza answered.

"Well, he drew his weapon on me earlier," I retorted.

"Are you for real?" Mendoza asked me concerned.

I began to backpedal. The last thing I needed was trouble with Hamilton and to be involved with filing an incident report. Especially when his big brother would just get the matter swept under the carpet and wind up making me the one that would get in trouble.

I began to stammer out some version of *"I was just kidding"* when a terrible odor overpowered my senses.

For the last decade of my life I had been around corpses at work. I had spent the entire afternoon bagging dead bodies that had been ripening in the sun for hours. The stink of decomposition was one that I had become accustomed to.

This scent was far more nauseating than anything I had ever smelled in my life. It was as if death itself had suddenly materialized around us.

I turned in the direction of the rancid stench and I couldn't believe my eyes.

I had just bagged and carried his dismembered body to the boat earlier, yet there he was, standing at the edge of the clearing, just beyond Officer Mendoza. The moonlight haloed him in a supernatural glow. He had literally been in pieces just a matter of minutes earlier yet there he stood before me.

Victor Crowley.

Nothing could have stopped what happened next. A freight train was leaving the station.

Crowley ran full steam towards Mendoza. The speed at which he moved was uncanny. For such a large man he was quick, almost doe-like. But there was no grace in his movement. It was pure rage and power personified. Mendoza turned towards the sound but didn't have time to reach for his weapon before Crowley ran into him.

No, that isn't precisely correct.
Crowley ran *through* him.

Mendoza didn't fall over. He didn't go flying through the air.

He *exploded.*

It was as though a bomb went off inside of his chest.

That bomb was Victor Crowley.

Blood and gore sprayed in all directions. A severed arm flipped through the air, the fingers on the hand moved as though it was trying to play a classical piece on an acoustic guitar.

Crowley slowed to a stop and angrily looked at the pieces of the body that lied in all directions. He walked over to Mendoza's head, still connected to the right shoulder and pectoral muscle. Bright yellow fat poked out from the torn flesh.

For those that haven't been privy to an autopsy, the color of body fat can be shocking. It's so bright and vibrant.

There is a theory in the medical world that a severed head can continue to see and react for up to twelve seconds. Of course there is no way to test this. It is pure theory. The eye and mouth movements can be an involuntary reaction to the trauma and nothing more than that. It's common for there to still be some residual energy stored. Cadavers have been known to twitch and move in the days following death sending many a med school student running for the hills. Behind the scenes we call that a "shake."

What startled me wasn't Mendoza's "shake." It was his eyes. They darted around, seeing everything, confused but also knowing. This was no involuntary reflex. He was aware of what had happened to him.

Did he feel pain? It didn't appear so. I'm sure the sudden shock would be enough to numb everything, plus most of the nerves were severed and lying in a thirty-foot radius. But he knew. He knew he was dying.

He looked directly at me.

I was staring at him and his eyes saw me. I'll never forget that glance. Thinking back it seemed like minutes passed as we looked at each other, but I know it was only a couple of seconds at most.

Victor Crowley picked up the head and partial torso. He stared into Mendoza's eyes. Thankfully I could no longer see his face from where I stood. Crowley sunk his thumbs into the eye sockets and pulled the head apart as though he was tearing open a piece of fruit. I could see the medulla oblongata peek out before

I saw the brain itself. Crowley grabbed the brain in his hand tearing it from the head. He cast the remnants away as though it was trash. He held the brain aloft. I wondered what he was going to do with it. The legend certainly didn't paint him as a cannibal. But the way he looked at Mendoza's brain, I half expected him to take a big bite out of it.

A man in tactical gear stepped out of the tree line beyond Crowley. The first of the cavalry had arrived.

"Freeze motherfucker!" the officer screamed as he drew his weapon. Crowley turned to him and in one motion threw the brain with all his might. It struck the officer in the neck and splattered all over his face, knocking him to the ground.

The officer dropped his gun, sat up and began pulling the viscera from his face while simultaneously spitting up the chunks of brain matter that had broken off into his open mouth. I could see the name on his vest. *Davis*.

Crowley ran at the man, letting out a loud roar. Right, when he reached him he kicked forward and Davis' head flew off high into the air. It cleared the tree line.

I'm not sure if it was ever found or not. It wouldn't surprise me if it is orbiting somewhere in space.

Blood spurted up from Davis' torn neck.

The sound of more officers rushing through the trees captured Crowley's attention. He stepped off into the brush towards the approaching officers and out of my view.

Had it not been for the large group of officers racing towards him and distracting him he likely would have charged at me next. He surely could have and it would have been over quickly.

That's the thing about Crowley. You're dead before you even realize death is imminent.

I stood there, in shock. I tried to scream to at least warn the approaching officers but my mouth was so dry that no sound could come out.

I had heard about Victor Crowley all my life and having seen his corpse earlier, I knew he was real, but seeing him in action was a whole different story. What he does… what he can do… it's *supernatural.*

I knew there was no fighting back.

I only had two options:

1. Escape the swamp. The boat was in the opposite direction from where he had just gone and I likely could have made it. But I couldn't leave people behind. I save lives. I help people.

2. Try to help and save as many people as I could and then hide. I just had to make it until dawn.

Victor Crowley's spirit only returned to roam the swamp at night. At least that's what the legend said and at this point, I now believed every word of it.

Gunshots and screaming erupted from the direction Crowley had just exited.

I distinctly heard Jim's gruff voice in the chorus of pained screams. It was too late for me to help them but I knew I could still try and warn the rest.

I looked at Davis' body. His radio was still attached to his shoulder.

I crawled on my belly over to his remains. Blood was still spurting out of his neck in geysers. I reached down and grabbed the radio when Davis' hand suddenly reached up and grabbed mine.

I screamed. This time the sound came out of my mouth.

I was trying to peel Davis' hand off of mine when I heard the unforgettable sound that will haunt me to my grave.

"Daaaaddddy...." Crowley called out into the night.

His ghostly wail filled every space of the swamp, momentarily silencing the insects in fear.

I could hear Crowley moving through the trees towards me.

He had heard my scream.

I would be next.

I tore Davis' hand free of mine, breaking a few of his lifeless fingers in the process. I looked around the clearing and realized I would not be able to run away in time. I was in no position to fight so I did the only thing I could do to preserve my safety.

I tried to hide.

I pulled Davis' body on top of mine. I closed my eyes and silently prayed Crowley would not notice me.

I could hear his footsteps as he walked past. He seemed to have missed me entirely.

I opened my eyes and stole a peek. It wasn't Victor Crowley. It was another officer. I eventually found out his name was Bennett.

He stared back at me with terror in his eyes while motioning for me to stay put.

Bennett took cover behind a nearby tree as his gun shook in his trembling hands.

I pulled Davis' body fully back over my own. From my point of view on the ground, I could see Bennett's boots.

That's when I noticed the second pair on the other side of the tree.

There wasn't even time for me to scream.

Crowley reached around and grabbed Bennett's arms with brute force, pulling him forward against the tree.

Bennett screamed and tried to pull back as his face was forced into the bark. Both of his arms came off as easily as you'd pluck a stem from an apple. Blood erupted from the torn shoulders as the sinew rippled in the breeze.

The momentum caused him to fall onto his back.

But his pain wasn't over yet.

Crowley, still standing behind the tree, bent down and grabbed Bennett's legs. He pulled him towards the tree again.

Bennett's genitals were crushed against the tree as Crowley reared back. The right leg came off as quickly as the two arms, while the left leg held strong as though it were the winning side of a wishbone.

A gunshot rang out and hit Crowley in the chest. I glanced over and saw another officer standing there. He stood and waited for a reaction from Crowley.

He got it.

It just wasn't what he expected.

Crowley nonchalantly reached behind his back and pulled a *hatchet* from his overalls.

It was only at this point that it dawned on me just what a bloodthirsty beast Crowley actually was. That hatchet had been on him the whole time but only now did he actually use it.

It's as if he preferred to tear his victims apart with his bare hands.

The officer moved to fire again but Crowley threw his hatchet directly into the man's chest, knocking him to the ground.

The man struggled for breath. I've seen MMA fights where someone lands a kick to the chest and sends someone sprawling. No kick could amount to the force behind Crowley's hatchet throw.

The man looked up to see Crowley standing above him, staring down. I saw what he was holding before the man could see it.

Crowley held *Bennett* in his hands.

He gripped the left leg, which was still attached to the armless torso. Somehow Bennett was still alive but he was in shock. He didn't scream. He didn't fight. He just hung there, suspended over the ground in Crowley's hands.

Crowley lifted Bennett up like a human meat cleaver. The resemblance in the moonlight was uncanny. Crowley swung his "man cleaver" in the air and brought it down onto the officer on the ground. The thud was loud and sickening. Crowley lifted Bennett up and delivered another blow.

Even missing his arms and one leg Bennett's body still had to weigh at least 125 pounds, yet Crowley ferociously swung him into the man on the ground over and over again.

After what seemed like a dozen blows, the two men's heads connected and exploded.

Another gunshot echoed in the swamp striking Crowley in the back. An officer moved towards him, firing again and again.

It did nothing more than piss Crowley off.

Crowley ran at the officer, driving his hand into the man's stomach. Blood flowed out of the wound as Crowley pushed his hand deep inside. The man screamed in pain as Crowley pulled his intestines out like he was cleaning a turkey.

With one final push, Crowley shoved his arm completely inside the man, plowing through the lungs and up through the chest. The man's head tilted back and his mouth opened as Crowley's hand popped out.

Even after all I had witnessed, I couldn't believe what I was seeing.

Crowley gripped the man's lower jaw from the inside and pulled it back. The jaw snapped as Crowley dragged it into the man's mouth and yanked it back down his throat. The man's neck stretched and distorted as he choked on his own jaw. The skin under the now missing chin was pulled inward, almost like a reverse zipper. The officer's chest and ribs caved in as Crowley pulled the jawbone into the abdominal area.

With one final heave, Crowley pulled the jaw out of the man's stomach, opening his torso wide and literally turning him inside out.

Somewhere in the trees, more officers began shouting and firing. Victor charged after them but from my position on the ground, I couldn't see what happened after that. I could only hear it.

I closed my eyes and waited for it to end.

After a few moments the swamp fell into a sickly silence. I dared not move. I focused on trying to breathe as slowly as possible. I could see the blood from Davis' body begin to pool up on the ground all around me.

It seemed like an eternity went by as I lay still on the wet ground beneath the corpse. With all of the disemboweled dead bodies all around me, the air was ripe with the stink of blood, feces, and urine. Eventually, the putrid smell of death began to overtake me.

I tried to only breathe through my mouth so that the smells wouldn't trigger my gag reflex and give away my hiding spot. I could feel mosquitoes biting my hands and my neck but I was helpless. I let them feed on my blood.

Something crawled into my mouth and I slowly began trying to push whatever it was back out with my tongue.

That's when I heard the loud thumps of his footsteps approaching again.

As hard as I tried to spit out the revolting insect inside of my mouth, whatever it was held on tightly inside. I could feel it crawling across my tongue. It was too long and had too many legs to be a basic spider. I just prayed that it wasn't poisonous.

With Crowley coming back I only had one option left.

I clenched down with my teeth and felt my mouth fill with the bitter fluid of the insect. I slowly swallowed it down. A small chunk of the exoskeleton caught on my uvula and tickled it. I fought to control my body's natural urge to vomit and for a few perilous seconds I feared I would begin retching. Through sheer will alone I was able to withstand the feeling.

Crowley's boots walked right up to where I was hiding. I held my breath and waited for my death, but it did not come.

It seemed like a full minute went by with him standing over me. His boot was only three inches from my face.

Suddenly he stepped away and walked back over to the officer he had beaten to death with Bennett's body. I watched as he leaned down and effortlessly yanked his hatchet out of the man's chest. He slid the weapon back into his bloodstained overalls and stormed off into the bushes.

It wasn't long before I heard his mournful cry again.

"...Daaadddyyy...."

He was getting further and further away but I was still too paralyzed with fear to move from my spot.

I'm not sure how long I actually waited there but it felt like hours. I wondered if anyone else was still alive. Minutes were passing without the sounds of screaming or gunfire. If anyone else had survived they would have had to be hiding like I was.

But that was merely the first wave. The real slaughter was yet to come.

How much longer until sunrise? Six hours? Seven? Beneath my corpse shelter claustrophobia began to set in. The pain from the mosquitoes feasting on my skin started to drive me insane.

I couldn't remain there and continue to be tortured much longer.

My mind turned to Sabrina. I re-lived the night that we first met, our first kiss, her hand in mine, our wedding day.

Things may have been difficult but I knew that she was waiting for me outside of that cursed swamp. I had spent the last two nights writing a new song for her and she was going to hear it.

When push comes to shove you have to ask yourself if you have what it takes to fight. Even when you know that you're most likely destined to lose.

I chose to fight. I was going to make a run for the boat even if it meant certain death.

That's when I heard more boats approaching. I listened as my heart pounded in my chest. Moments later I heard voices.

Help had arrived.

I crawled out of my hiding spot and ran into what looked like a small army. There were at least a dozen heavily armed SWAT team members flanked by half a dozen state and local police officers. They all had their weapons trained on me.

"Don't shoot!" I cried out.

I recognized Sheriff Fowler and expected him to be in charge but I was wrong. A huge, bald-headed man standing at the front of the group was leading their rescue expedition. While I didn't know his name at the time, I've since learned it was Lieutenant Tyler Hawes.

He was incredibly intense with an overt machismo that radiated off of him in waves. Under any other circumstances, I would have found Hawes' fearless and militant arrogance comforting but I knew what he and his team of soldiers were walking into. I let him know that we needed to get out of there immediately.

Unfortunately for everyone involved, Hawes wasn't going to listen to a single thing I said. Even while standing there in a literal forest of gore, the lieutenant scoffed at my account of what had happened and *who* was actually responsible for it.

Sheriff Fowler had been a local for almost his entire life and I knew he was quite familiar with the Victor Crowley legend. After all, his ex-wife was Amanda Fowler, the self-proclaimed "Crowley expert" who had virtually thrown away her career as a legitimate journalist years earlier by publishing a story that boldly proclaimed the Victor Crowley legend to be real. Amanda's story had even gone as far as to accuse Louisiana's politicians and other authorities of covering it up. She was fired immediately afterward and she had become a joke in the journalism world overnight.

As much as Sheriff Fowler may not have wanted to accept what I was saying, I could tell that his gut knew better than to doubt me. Victor Crowley may have been a sensitive subject for him but one look at the war zone we were standing in and he knew that we were all in over our heads. He attempted to call for help but Hawes tore the radio from his hand and canceled the call. He would not allow anyone to embarrass him by requesting back-up. *He* was the back-up.

I let Hawes know that his ego was going to get us all killed but he wouldn't listen to me.

A young deputy who I later came to know as Schneiderman challenged Hawes. He clearly believed in the legend of Victor Crowley as he had brought a duffle bag on the mission that was filled with his own arsenal of high tech weaponry. Schneiderman may have been a gun nut, but he appeared to be the only other rational person among us. He echoed my pleas to Hawes that we were in terrible danger.

At one point during their argument Schneiderman pointed out a pair of testicles that were hanging from a nearby tree like a grotesque Christmas ornament. Still, Hawes refused to accept that we were up against anything that he couldn't handle.

When Schneiderman quit and tried to walk back to the boats Hawes pinned him against a tree and threatened him.

I tried again to make Hawes understand that we weren't dealing with a man but a supernatural monster. I told him how Crowley had taken every bullet and just kept coming. I warned him that if we didn't leave immediately that we would all surely die, too.

As if on cue there was suddenly a noise in the bushes directly behind us. The SWAT team and police deputies turned in unison and began to fire into the bushes.

Once the barrage of firepower stopped, Hawes walked over to investigate what exactly had made the noise that scared everyone.

He held up the carcass of a raccoon.

Hawes actually found their mistake amusing and began to joke about it when Crowley's voice cut through the night air.

"Daaaaaddddy," Victor Crowley cried.

The terrifying sound made most of the team member's hearts stop. My own heart included. I may have already been familiar with the chilling sound of Victor Crowley's mournful wail but my fear of it wasn't diminished in any way. It's an unholy sound. Not one you could ever get used to hearing.

"Daaaaaddddy," Victor Crowley wailed again.

His voice was pained. It was filled with anguish.

It was also close.

The fireworks show that the SWAT team had set off laying waste to the harmless raccoon had brought death right to us.

I begged the others to run back to the boats but Hawes fearlessly and foolishly lead everyone forward. We came out of the bushes into a small clearing.

There before us was the old Crowley house. I had removed a few bodies from in and around the property earlier in the day. The place was cursed.

You could feel it.

Hawes signaled for the team to spread out in attack formation. One group remained with their guns trained on the house while another took position in front of an old shed on the property.

Hawes was poised to strike first.

He didn't get the chance.

Crowley threw a fishing spear through the chest of an officer and yanked him inside the darkness of the shed. His screams were cut short instantly.

As the mayhem and panic began to break out, a female deputy that was trying to flee from the shed was struck with a spiked fishing hook in her shoulder and dragged onto the ground. As Crowley began to pull her back into the shed the other officers all opened fire in the space above her. They must have shot hundreds of bullets into that shed but it was useless.

Fearing that she would be hit by one of the bullets I moved into position to throw myself on top of her, shield her, and pull her away but Sheriff Fowler beat me to it. Seeing that he couldn't win at Crowley's tug of war he fired his weapon and severed the rope that Crowley was dragging her by.

Unfortunately, all Crowley had to do at that point was reach out and grab her. He pulled her inside of the shed where we heard him tear her apart.

A second later, Crowley violently threw both of the dead officers' corpses through the walls of the shed.

"Fire!" I yelled, knowing that with Crowley pinned inside of the shed this was our best shot. Crowley may have gone un-phased by handguns but the SWAT team was packing all kinds of automatic rifles and shotguns. I had not yet seen him try and take a stand against *this* kind of firepower.

They lit up the shed with all their might.

How Victor Crowley was able to escape I'll never know but somehow he was suddenly *behind* us.

He tackled one of the SWAT team members. Unable to shoot at Crowley without risking hitting the officer, several SWAT team members charged and began striking him with their weapons. He tossed them off like ragdolls before lifting up the officer he had tackled.

Crowley held the man above his head and effortlessly pulled him in *half* right before our eyes.

As the officers on the ground got back up to fight, Crowley tore through them. It was all a blur as he began to hack everyone apart. Heads and other limbs went flying under the punishment of his hatchet. He threw one of the men onto the ground and stomped his head like a grape.

Everyone went back to shooting at Crowley until they were out of ammunition.

In the most over the top display of bravado and stupidity I will ever see in my life, Hawes stepped forward and engaged Crowley in a fistfight. He was obviously no match for the monstrous Crowley who ended the brawl before it could even begin.

He punched into Hawes' stomach, grabbed onto his spine, and with just a couple of tugs pulled it right out of his torso with his skull still connected. The skin of the Lieutenant's empty head was pulled inside of his own body. The most macho man I had ever encountered was literally rendered spineless.

By this point, it had become evident to the few of us who were still standing that guns were not going to stop Victor Crowley.

Deputy Schneiderman had something else in mind.

He pulled a bazooka out of his duffle bag. I've been told that the correct term is a rocket launcher but I'm going to call it as I saw it. It was a *bazooka*.

By this point, Crowley was tearing apart an officer directly in front of the house. Schneiderman shot the rocket straight at him and the old Crowley house exploded in flames.

The sound of the explosion was deafening. Pieces of the house flew all around us. The ringing in my ears took me right back to the motorcycle accident I had witnessed as a teenager. The very same accident that had set me on the path that led me to this terrible night.

I surveyed the damage. Victor Crowley was nowhere to be seen. Schneiderman began to cheer. There was a split second where even I almost started to celebrate, too.

Nothing could have survived an explosion like that.

But of course, Crowley did.

Somehow he did.

Victor Crowley threw a flaming chunk of wood from the burning house and speared Schneiderman directly in the back, knocking him down.

A female SWAT member named Dougherty fearlessly rushed in to try to help the young deputy but Crowley backhanded her aside and sent her flying. I motioned to Sheriff Fowler and he began to fire at Crowley as a distraction. I rushed in and helped Dougherty to her feet as the three of us ran for our lives.

I'm not sure what exactly happened to Schneiderman after that. As we sprinted back towards the boats I could briefly hear him screaming.

Then we heard nothing.

As we tore through the trees I ran straight into "what's-his-name" knocking both of us down onto the ground. Of *course* out of everyone who had been sent to their untimely deaths that night "what's-his-name", the guy who only ever got in the way and messed things up, had somehow also survived!

I helped him to his feet and told him to follow us back to the boats.

Never one to listen to directions "what's-his-name" took off running in the very direction we were running away from. Sheriff Fowler shouted to him but he didn't listen. He just kept running. It was the last time I'd ever see him.

For the life of me I still couldn't tell you "what's-his-name's" name.

I led Sheriff Fowler and Dougherty to the ambulance boat. I knew it was our best chance of survival.

There was one big problem with my plan, however.

I didn't have the keys.

My co-workers' constant running racist joke about never letting me near the keys was now about to cost us our lives.

We changed course to Sheriff Fowler's boat but it was too late.

Crowley was blocking our path.

With nowhere left to turn we took shelter inside the ambulance boat and barricaded the door behind us. Crowley came barreling down against it just a second later. He banged and banged on the door trying to tear it down.

For a brief moment, we were somewhat safe.

Crowley ferociously pounded on the ambulance boat walls sending items flying off of the shelves. Glass bottles shattered to the floor and various liquids spilled by our feet under the punishment Crowley delivered to the steel walls.

Sheriff Fowler used the onboard radio to call for help. When the operator answered and asked what the circumstances of the emergency were, the sheriff hesitated. Even though numerous emergency calls had already been made from the swamp that night (hell, that was why wave after wave of victims had walked right into the slaughterhouse), Sheriff Fowler knew he had to say something that the person on the other end of the line would respond to quickly and without question.

He said there was a gunman firing at us and that we were pinned down inside the boat. I suppose being able to think that quickly under duress is what makes someone capable of becoming a sheriff. Had he started trying to explain that Victor Crowley was massacring all of us there would have been questions asked, doubt raised, and time wasted. By declaring that we were taking fire from a crazed gunman the response was swift. We were told that the National Guard would be on their way with a rescue helicopter within minutes.

The only problem was that we didn't have minutes.

That's when Crowley stopped attacking the boat.

There was silence.

The three of us froze as we listened for a sign of what was happening outside of the boat and what Crowley's next move might be. I looked over and saw Randy lying there. Even without his face, I could recognize my friend. I wondered who would bag and tag his body.

We heard the sound of a cable pulling followed by a motor sputtering to life. Suddenly sparks began to fly into the boat as Crowley used the belt sander I had unfortunately left on the dock to saw his way inside. There was nowhere for us to go. He was cutting through fast.

The sander chewed through the boat's wiring and the power went out. The only light left inside the boat came from the glowing sparks that showered all around us.

With all of the flammable materials scattered on the boat's floor, I fully expected a spark to land on something and start a fire. Being burned alive is one of the most painful ways to die.

But what was coming for us was far worse.

Suddenly the belt sander stopped. There was silence. I noticed a hammer on the boat floor. It must have fallen out of the toolkit when it toppled to the ground under Crowley's attack against the walls. A hammer wouldn't do much but at least it was something to fight back with.

As I reached for it Crowley grabbed ahold of my shirt and pulled me towards him. I was flung against the wall like a plastic action figure under his sheer power. Dougherty began beating on Crowley's arm with the hammer like a crazed mad woman and after a few seconds he released me from his grasp and went back to using the sander once again.

His sander chewed through the steel wall of the boat, sending sparks flying all around us. With the stench of death filling my nostrils I knew someone had to do something fast. Someone had to stand up and fight back against the monster. And that someone was me.

Once again the sanding stopped.

The hole was now big enough for a person to look outside. Though I knew leaning out with Crowley there was a risky move, we needed to find out what was happening and why he had stopped.

I volunteered but before I could move from my spot, we heard other voices yelling in the distance.

"Amanda!" Sheriff Fowler exclaimed.

I assumed that the sheriff was merely hearing things in his panicked state but he was sure that he could hear his ex-wife somewhere outside of the boat.

He foolishly thrust his head through the hole to call for her and Crowley grabbed ahold of him in an instant. Dougherty and I tried to pull Fowler back inside. It was like some kind of morbid tug of war over a human being.

The sound of the sander grinding through Sheriff Fowler's head filled the dark ambulance boat as his body convulsed in shock. His headless body fell back inside, hosing us down with the Sheriff's blood.

In that instant, I could only think about what happens when a chicken has its head cut off. How its wings continue to flap and its body continues to run around for a short period of time before finally accepting death's embrace. Sheriff Fowler's body did the same thing. I could feel the vomit rise in the back of my throat but I swallowed the hot bile back down.

Moments passed and there was silence again from outside. Crowley seemed to be playing a game with us.

Dougherty and I sat paralyzed in our opposite corners. I wondered how much longer it would be before the National Guard would get there. Though it felt like several hours had passed since the Sheriff called for help, in reality, it couldn't have been more than two minutes.

I wondered how we would get to the helicopter if we were still alive when it did finally arrive. Could we even take off? What had the sheriff's ex-wife been doing out there and how and when did she arrive? Nothing about her presence added up or made even a lick of sense. I was so deep into the nightmare that I had given up on trying to rationalize any of it.

Dougherty motioned to Sheriff Fowler's gun on the floor of the boat. I shook the idea off and whispered to her not to even think about it. What good was the gun anyway? Victor Crowley had already been shot with a bazooka. The weapon would do no good.

She wouldn't listen though.

"I still have ammo," she proclaimed to me.

In her helpless fear, I think she only wanted the security of the useless firearm in her hands.

Despite my pleas to stay where she was Dougherty slowly made her way against the boat wall and crawled directly beneath the gaping hole Crowley had created with the belt sander.

I could see what was going to happen but I was powerless to stop it. I wanted to shove

Dougherty away but my body felt like it was moving underwater.

Crowley reached through and grabbed her arm. She screamed as he frantically pulled her into the hole. Over and over again he slammed her into the shredded metal gap. I waited for her arm to be ripped from her body but what actually happened was far more brutal.

As Crowley pulled her out of the boat her flesh caught along the jagged edge of the hole and she was peeled apart like a banana. Her intestines fell in a steaming pile as Crowley dragged what was left intact of her body outside. Dougherty was nothing more than a pile of guts on the ambulance boat floor.

By Crowley violently pulling Dougherty's body through the boat wall he had now made the hole big enough for him to get through. I knew my time had run out and that I was next.

I had tried to save whomever I could and failed.

Now death was coming for me.

As I hunkered down and braced myself for the end I noticed something on the floor in Dougherty's remains.

The belt sander.

Crowley must have dropped it during the struggle to pull her outside.

I didn't hesitate. I reached into the pile of warm intestines and lifted the sander up in my hands. I pulled the cord to try and start it but it was so slippery with blood and viscera that the cord merely kept slapping against the small gas compartment with each pull.

Crowley began to force himself through the wall of the boat, bending back the steel under the weight of his massive body. His rotting stench permeated the stagnant air around me.

His head and shoulders were inside the boat when the belt sander sputtered to life in my hands.

I pressed the whirring sander into his disfigured face and I was instantly showered with a mixture of blood and teeth. Adrenaline took control of my body. I screamed and leaned into him as hard as I could. I felt the sander begin to shred the bone of his enormous skull when he finally went limp and fell down on the dock somewhere outside of the boat.

I heard an enormous splash as his lifeless body rolled into the swamp. I didn't see what became of him but from the hissing and splashing sounds I heard, I could only imagine that Crowley's body became a meal for the many gators that had gathered to feed off of the bodies outside.

His body was never found.

Not a trace.

The next thing I knew the spotlight from the rescue helicopter above was shining down inside the boat. I stepped out and began to wave my arms as I screamed for help.

I survived.

Chapter Eight

The Arrest

Thirteen is considered an unlucky number and in my personal experience it certainly seemed to be.

My mother was diagnosed with cancer on September 13th, 2006.

Sabrina and I were together for thirteen years.

It was thirteen years between O.J. Simpson's "trial of the century" and my own "trial of *this* century."

I was arrested on March 13th, 2007.

On the day of my arrest, I was sitting on the couch quietly contemplating my life. The last few days had been such an emotional and physical whirlwind that even the wide array of medications my doctor had me on couldn't help. Until my mother passed away I had never been seriously medicated in my life. Less than two weeks later I was now on pills to sleep, pills to stay calm, pills to function, and pills to try and stop the screaming in my head. I was so drugged up that most of the time I could barely keep my head up.

Everything felt like one big blur.

My mother's funeral... the argument with Sabrina about the abortion... the massacre in the swamp... being rescued by the helicopter... waking up in the hospital... giving my statement to the police... Sabrina driving me home... the news cameras... seeing my image all over the television...

I was in such a haze that sometimes it was hard to distinguish which parts of the nightmare were real and which parts I was dreaming. Sometimes I couldn't even tell when I was awake or when I was asleep.

The country was obsessed with what the media had dubbed "The Honey Island Swamp Massacre." Every headline was a reminder of the horror I had experienced. The fact that I was somehow still alive made the whole ordeal even more difficult for me to digest.

The clinical term is "survivor's guilt" and I was suffocating in its vice-like grip.

So many people had lost their lives, many that were my colleagues and friends. It was an unfathomable ordeal that of course, everyone couldn't get enough of. It was O.J. all over again.

I couldn't step foot outside of the house without a constant bombardment of reporters and those that were just interested in catching a glimpse of me. I just wanted to grieve, to move on with my life and most importantly to reconnect with Sabrina.

She and I had already been struggling to reignite our marriage before the massacre but now we had become complete strangers. A rigid coldness had crept between us like a winter breeze through a cracked bedroom window.

The night that she had picked me up from the hospital I poured my heart out to her about everything I had experienced in the swamp. I was in and out of consciousness and would trail off at times since I was heavily medicated. I remember her listening and not judging. She even held my hand at one point. I thought it might be the beginning of our reconciliation.

Since that night she had virtually made herself invisible to me. She was always at work and when she did come home she barely said two words to me. The loneliness began to sweep me up in a wave of despair. I didn't know how I could possibly get through this without her.

I made up my mind. I wasn't going to let one more day go by without confronting her about avoiding me when I needed her most.

I heard the familiar sound of Sabrina's keys in the front door. I glanced at the clock surprised to see what time it was. My day had drifted due to the medication I had taken. I wasn't expecting her for a couple more hours and figured I'd have plenty of time to clear my head.

I rose and took a deep breath. For the first time in our marriage I was going to stand up for myself and say what *I* needed.

Sabrina stepped inside and closed the door.

"We need to talk," I said quickly, hoping that I wouldn't lose my nerve.

"Yes we do, Andrew. Why don't you have a seat?" She replied, motioning to the couch.

"I don't want to sit down," I said as I stepped towards her.

She took a step back and for the first time in our marriage I saw a glint of fear in her eyes.

"I have to tell you something," she said.

"I'm the one that is going to do the talking this time Sabrina," I replied.

"Okay," she muttered.

I wanted to say so much but I struggled to find the right words. I looked into her eyes and my resolve began to melt. I didn't want to fight. We had done enough of that. I just wanted her to show me some sort of affection.

I reached out to take her hand and she pulled away, bumping into the table by the door. The usual stack of unopened mail that was always sitting there fell to the ground.

Including the letter opener that had been left on top of it all.

I absentmindedly bent down and picked it up.

"I'm going to move out for awhile," she said.

"What?" I replied, shocked.

Sabrina took a deep breath…

"I want a separation," she blurted out.

I stood up quickly, unable to fully process what I had just heard. With the meds still coursing through my blood, suddenly standing made me dizzy. The room spun around me as I felt the blood rush from my face. I fell back and knocked over a lamp. It crashed to the floor and loudly shattered.

"How can you do this to me at a time like this?" I asked.

"You're not the person I married," she replied sadly.

"Me?!" I said, angrily. "Oh, you're right. It's totally my *fault*. *I* did this."

"I'm sorry," she said, as she looked from my eyes to the door.

"You can't leave-," was all I got out before she opened the door.

A man entered the house with a camera on his shoulder.

It was a local cameraman. I can still see the WDSU station letters on the camera.

Sabrina's station.

He stepped out of the doorway, stood behind the couch and pointed the camera at me. It was a complete invasion of privacy.

"What are you doing? You can't come in here," I said, anger flashing across my face.

This was my sanctuary. My home was the one place that the media had to leave me alone in the wake of what I had lived through.

"GET THE FUCK OUT OF HERE!" I screamed at the man.

Three FBI agents, two males, and a female stepped inside.

"Good. You're here. This news guy just barged in. I want him to leave," I said, stepping towards them.

I still hadn't put it all together.

Denial can be so strong.

The FBI agents looked at Sabrina.

"It's okay," Sabrina said, "he's with me."

I looked at her, confusion spreading across my face like wildfire. "What's going on?"

I didn't understand what was happening then, but I do now. I was going down and Sabrina was simply making sure that she didn't go down with me. Self-preservation was always her game and she would do anything she could to make sure that she didn't lose the career that she had worked so hard to build for herself.

The lead FBI agent stepped forward and pulled out his handcuffs.

"Andrew Yong, we have a warrant for your arrest."

"For *what*?" I asked incredulously.

"For the murders in Honey Island Swamp," he replied.

I stepped back out of shock and stumbled once more. It just didn't make sense. How could they think *I* did it? It was unfathomable.

"Hold on a second," I said as I held up my hands. "There's been a mistake."

"He's got a knife!" The female agent yelled.

I looked at the letter opener I was holding and opened my mouth to speak.

Before I could, the lead agent tackled me to the ground and rolled me over on my stomach.

I lifted my head up to try to talk some sense into him.

The female agent rushed over and put her knee on the back of my head, pushing me flat against the wood floor. The pain was immediate and I felt blood begin to flow from a gash that was created above my right eye.

"You have the right to remain silent, everything you say can and will be used against you in the court of law," she said as she slapped handcuffs on me.

"Please! You're making a mistake," I blurted out, the fog finally beginning to clear.

"You have the right to an attorney. If you don't have one then one will be appointed to you."

The FBI agents pulled me up to my feet as blood ran down into my eye.

"Do you understand your rights?" The lead agent asked.

I looked from the agents, to the cameraman, and finally at Sabrina.

"You knew?" I asked.

"You're sick, Andrew," she replied. "You need help."

"Pick up the weapon," the lead agent said to the female agent.

Weapon. As if a letter opener is a weapon. I saw real weapons in the swamp and this was laughable.

"Yes sir," she said, as she put on latex gloves.

"Let's go," he said to me, "and don't pull any shit, you son of a bitch."

They led me past Sabrina out the front door. There was an immediate rush of activity as cameras flashed and news reports went live. The locals that had gathered outside took it all in. Many were neighbors that I knew well; some I considered to be my friends. I looked for their support, but instead saw perplexed looks. From behind, I heard the cameraman speak to Sabrina.

"No one's gonna dare think you're still tied to that psycho now," he said unable to conceal the excitement in his voice. "You're safe."

Between the utter shock and blood running down my face, I realize that I looked horrific. Still, there was no way anyone could really believe I did anything wrong. How could they? They knew about the legend. Everyone around here did. I knew I could count on them coming to the true realization.

A gasp went through the crowd as the female agent walked out of the house with the letter opener in a plastic bag. She held it up, overtly grandiose and making sure that the cameras all got a shot of it. The faces of my friends and neighbors changed. Anger took over their expressions.

The lead agent shoved me into the back of his car and slammed the door. I looked out the window as people crowded around taking pictures. Some cursed at me.

Beyond them, I could see Sabrina standing in our doorway. She looked at me before taking a microphone from the cameraman. She did what she had done best ever since we got married.

She turned her back on me.

I sat in the backseat of the cruiser and wondered how it had come to this. I pride myself on being a good person.

How could this happen to *me*?

It just didn't make sense.

Do I look like the kind of guy that could brutally murder forty or so people over a weekend? We're not talking run-of-the-mill murder here. People weren't shot with an assault rifle or even stabbed with a knife. They were torn apart limb from limb.

"You're going to fry for this," the agent said, as he steered the car through traffic on our way to the station. He was seething in anger.

I don't blame him for that. Over half of the people that perished in the swamp were police officers. That isn't something the law takes lightly.

"I should just take you out to Honey Island Swamp and put a bullet in your head. Save the taxpayers all their hard earned money," he spat, through grinding teeth.

"I didn't do this," I replied.

"Sure you did, and we have the evidence to back it up."

"That's impossible," I said.

He did not reply. He just kept driving.

I sat back and wondered what this "evidence" could possibly be. I understood that the victims' families and the general public wanted answers that they could accept. It was now the law's job to deliver justice. But they would need a motive, a witness, or a murder weapon in order to pin this on me. None of which existed.

And why had it taken them a week to charge me? None of it made sense.

My thoughts drifted to Sabrina. I wondered how she could live with herself after doing this to me.

Sabrina couldn't have possibly believed that I did it. No way. She knew me, more than anyone else. She knew I wasn't capable of such a thing. I didn't even kill spiders. I let them go outside in the bushes. I had told her the whole story about what Victor Crowley did. She might not have believed me, but there is no conceivable way she could think I was the maniac that slaughtered all of those people.

I tried to remain positive that this was a giant misunderstanding and I would soon be free to go.

There was no way I was going to spend a night in jail.

I was escorted through the station where I recognized a handful of faces. People that had worked with me for years and who knew just what a solid and reliable EMT I was.

The familiar faces all looked away from me in disgust.

I was put in an empty cell to wait in until they could put me through the booking process. I sat down on the bed and sat motionless. It was as though paralysis had taken over. Deputies strolled by off and on and stole looks at me. No one actually talked to me. They just wanted to get a look at “the monster.” Life seemed to be moving in slow motion.

At some point, I stood up to wash the blood off my face in the sink.

“You the dude that killed everyone?” A male voice said, from the neighboring cell.

I tried to ignore him. There was no sense in conversing with an actual criminal. He deserved to be there not me. I wanted nothing to do with him.

He didn’t take the hint.

“Hey man. Don’t be a dick. You’re him, right?”

“I’m innocent,” I replied, turning to him.

The man stood at the bars grinning at me. He was chubby, bald and had a smile that hinted at menace.

“I know you are,” he said. “It was Victor Crowley, wasn’t it? Reverend Zombie tried to hire a whole group of us to hunt for Crowley last weekend. I knew something was going down.”

“Who’s Reverend Zombie?” I asked.

“He runs a voodoo shop in the quarter. Dude’s weird and shady as hell. I just went to listen to his offer cause he was giving out free cookies. No way was I ever gonna go out there. I ain't dumb."

"He led a hunting party out there?" I asked. "You can help me. Please! What do you know about Crowley?"

"I know everything about everything, Bro. I know it all."

The man seemed crazy. But he clearly had information that could help my case.

"You have to tell me everything you know," I excitedly said.

The man looked around, leaned against the bars and whispered.

"Can you help me?"

"Sure. Help you how?"

The man waved me closer before speaking.

"I need to get back to my spaceship."

"What?' I asked, deflated.

"They're trying to hold me here so that they can probe me again. I need to get back to my planet, Bro."

"Shut the fuck up, Louis," an officer said as he walked past the cell.

The man shot him a dirty look and went back to his bed.

"I get a phone call, right?" I asked, as I stood up and walked over to the cell door.

"You aren't getting shit," the agent said, as he continued on his way.

The man in the cell next to me laughed. I looked over at him and he laid some prophetic wisdom on me.

"You ain't going anywhere. Welcome to your new home. Courtesy flush or I'll piss on you while you sleep."

He was absolutely right. It was quite some time before I was able to see any sort of freedom. And to be honest, it may have been a good thing. I was now a pariah to the community and would be the most hated man in America by morning. If given the chance the officers holding me would have lynched me.

They needed someone to blame, a villain. Too many lives were lost. I was being set up to be their sacrificial lamb. It was better to take me down than to admit the truth. This allowed them to sleep at night. Their local ghost story could remain a legend.

I sat back down on the bed and held my head in my hands.

I'd like to tell you that I was tough. That I remained stoic knowing that the truth would come out. I'd like to tell you that but I can't.

Tears were shed, though I did my best to hide them. I didn't know much about jail, but I knew that's not something you let people see, especially someone who had just threatened to urinate on you.

So I cried and thought about Sabrina.

Was she crying? I wanted her to.

There was also something else I wanted.

I wanted my Mom.

I had told the authorities the truth when I first got off of the helicopter that terrible night. They all knew the legend. You couldn't live here and *not* know it. Some of it changed depending on the person telling it. Like everything in life, there were embellishments. But the basics always remained the same. Victor Crowley was real.

At the beginning of this chapter, I mentioned the number thirteen and how it's clearly unlucky for me. There's something that just dawned on me though. If you count the letters in his name, the evil monster that caused all of this, they number thirteen.

V I C T O R C R O W L E Y.

I, Survivor.

Chapter Nine

The Arraignment

My arraignment took place on March 15th, 2007. To say I was still shocked that this was actually happening is an understatement. At no point did I feel that this would go forward. There was no evidence that I was involved in the crimes perpetrated by Victor Crowley. I kept waiting for everyone to come to their senses.

I guess it was easier to blame me than to try and explain Louisiana's local boogeyman. I was made of flesh, bone, and cells. I was a villain that could easily be accepted by the masses and a trial of this size was always about the masses.

Locally, many believed that Victor Crowley was real. They grew up with the belief that he exists or had existed in some form at some point. Legends usually have some basis in fact. But this trial captivated the world in a way no other trial had since O.J.. There had never been such a gruesome and horrific murder spree.

I am an unwilling celebrity. To this day I can't go anywhere without someone recording me and taking a picture.

Sometimes they just shout "murderer".

This is the hardest thing for me to come to terms with. I became a medic in order to help people and save lives. It's my passion, my love, and what I thought my purpose in life was. Now the career I loved so much has been taken from me.

To this day I'm branded as the most evil being to ever walk the face of the earth.

I've learned to try and ignore the nasty comments that I constantly get but I am a human being. My experiences were and continue to be real.

Strangers joke around about what I've been through but every joke hurts deeply. Every comment reminds me how I've lost everything.

I hadn't seen Sabrina since the day I was arrested. It hurt that she had betrayed me the way she did but I know that she was just trying to protect herself, her precious image, and her career. By broadcasting her stunt it let everyone know that their beloved Sabrina Caruthers from the TV screen was not standing by her husband the mass murderer. She made sure that the world watched her help the authorities take me down.

But what would she do once the evidence proved I was innocent and I was exonerated? How would the beloved celebrity who so publicly betrayed her innocent husband regain the love of her audience at that point? What would her ratings have to say about her integrity then? Once I was set free and seen as the victim I really am in all of this, Sabrina's career would be finished.

On a positive note, perhaps Sabrina's exile from television would bring her back down to earth again. Once she was no longer daytime talk show royalty she would turn back into the woman I had fallen in love with in the first place.

And when my dear wife ultimately fell from grace I would still be there to catch her. Even after all she had done to me, I would still have it in my heart to forgive her.

That's love.

And it was just like my mother had told me. In the end love is all that matters.

I don't give up. It's not in my nature. It's why I'm still here today. I was still alive. Almost everyone I knew wasn't. Every breath I took was one more than they were afforded.

But I earned my life. Even though it should be a better life than I've been forced to endure.

Only one other person has ever survived Victor Crowley, but you won't read about her anywhere.

She's the mystery girl who originally reported the dead bodies out in Honey Island Swamp.

She had to have told *someone* at Jefferson Parish PD what really happened or there would be no reason for us to have been sent to Honey Island Swamp to pick up the pieces in the first place.

And if the girl knew about the bodies that means that she had somehow managed to escape Victor Crowley. But no one will even acknowledge her existence now.

I know she exists because that day in Honey Island Swamp I overheard Jim and Hamilton discuss Jefferson Parish PD having a girl in custody.

Originally the story I heard was that the girl who tipped them off was being held while they investigated the crime scene, but she was never charged or booked. Somehow she mysteriously vanished from her cell never to be seen or heard from again.

Someone in the Jefferson Parish PD has to be covering up her release.

If you look at the police department's records *now*, they merely list that a "Jane Doe" walked in, gave an anonymous tip about the bodies, and walked out of the station.

You're trying to tell me that there isn't something shady going on there?

Someone out there has to know who she is. *Someone* knows the truth. But they won't talk.

In the hopes that the mystery girl reads this:

Jane Doe,

For a long time, I searched for you in my quest for vindication. You know the truth of what happened in that swamp as you experienced it firsthand. You know what I was up against. What it took to survive. I have been angry with you for quite some time. I held onto the hate, knowing that you could have come forward and helped me when I was unjustly facing the death penalty. Did you watch my trial? How could you not step forward to share whatever you knew? You could have saved me a lifetime of pain and anguish. Yet you chose to stay in the shadows.

I used to question my own sanity. There were moments in my life where I blamed you as much as I blamed Victor Crowley. Sure, you didn't chase me through the swamp on that path of destruction but you did allow the destruction of my life to continue unabated.

I cursed you on those dark lonely nights I spent in jail.

Where did you go?

I've wanted to find you, to scream at you, to take it out on you. I wanted to take it out on someone. I've been the world's whipping post for all of this.

Have you been able to get your life back on track?

I wonder.

Do you still wake up at night, in a cold sweat, hearing him call for his Daddy?

I do.

I've held so much hate in my heart for you over the years. Every attempt to find you has led to a dead end. It's as though you have vanished.

I've come to a profound realization while writing this book.

I'm not angry with you anymore. I'm envious of you.

I'm sure your life isn't all roses. I know that you must have to deal with the psychological ramifications of the Crowley experience just like I have to. The difference is that you've been able to do it without the world judging your every move and blaming you for what that monster did. That is my burden to carry alone.

But I no longer fault you.

Had you come forward it still wouldn't have changed anyone's mind. After all, I was proven innocent beyond a shadow of a doubt yet they still blame, hate, and crucify me to this day. Had you come forward the only thing it would have accomplished is destroying your life too.

I don't wish that on you. I don't wish that on anyone.

You are the only person in the world that can relate to what I experienced. You survived. That's why I still want to find you. Just once I want to talk to someone that believes me. I want to look into your eyes and see recognition there. You know the truth.

Victor Crowley is real.

I ask that you find it in your heart to reach out to me. I want to hear your story. There has to be a reason we both survived. I won't drag you through the mud. I just want a moment of clarity in the hopes of releasing some of the anguish I've been unable to let go of.

I try so hard to forget, as I'm sure you do. But I can't. It's always there. Maybe together we can find a way to cast it aside. If anything I will finally be able to assure myself that I'm not alone.

Andrew

The arraignment was held in New Orleans. Originally they thought the trial would be held there but it was later moved. There was no way the prosecution was ever going to allow anyone that believed the legend of Victor Crowley to set foot on the jury. I know that's not publicly discussed, but it's the truth.

Fair trial my ass.

The State needed a conviction for this massacre. There were too many dead, too many families destroyed. The actual trial would ultimately be held in Bossier County, far away from Honey Island Swamp.

The arraignment was my first taste of what was to come.

I had hoped that I could change out of my orange jumpsuit into some real clothes. I didn't want people to see me that way. I was laughed at when I requested my own clothes, but they said they'd bring me something else to wear.

It ended up being a bulletproof vest.

"What's this for?" I asked as it was pulled over my head.

"Protection," the deputy said.

"From what?"

"You'll see," he said with a smirk.

And I did.

The cameras started flashing and the mob moved forward. I could hear yelling and screaming. It was as though a tsunami of hate crashed into me.

"Murderer!"

"Motherfucker!"

"Bastard!"

Some in the angry mob held up photos of the victims. I didn't recognize most of the faces pictured. I would later. It was a tactic the prosecution used. They inundated the jury with pictures of the victims. Their smiling faces grinning for retribution. And that was what the trial was really about.

All I could see heading to my arraignment was the hatred everyone already had for me.

It hurt me to my core.

I knew I was innocent. It was a miracle that I had survived. I wasn't looking for praise or fame. I just wanted to get back to my life. At the very least I wanted to stop being falsely blamed for all of it.

The crowd reached for me. The anger permeating from their combined anguish clouded their judgment.

The guards shoved me in a van and we were off to the courthouse. The ride was short but to me it felt like an eternity.

I wanted to see Sabrina so badly. I needed to know how she was holding up. I longed to see sadness and regret on her face.

I entered the courtroom and looked around. It was a full house. I was happy to see my father sitting among the spectators. I gave him the best smile I could summon up. I didn't wait to see if he returned it. I wish I had. I wish that I would have told him I loved him.

My focus turned back to finding Sabrina in the crowd. I scanned the courtroom for her as I was led to a small podium. She had to be there. I couldn't see her though. I was so intent on getting a glimpse that I wasn't paying attention to what was going on in front of me.

The arraignment had begun.

The proceedings were played out to a national audience and I wasn't leaving a good impression. My eyes were darting all over the place. Each sweep of the audience would result in me becoming more distraught. Was Sabrina really not there? I couldn't fathom that. I must have been missing her somehow. I'd scan again, each time more and more obsessed with finding her.

Sabrina wasn't there.

I entered my plea of not guilty and of course I was immediately denied bail. In a murder case involving so many victims there was no way bail would have been an option.

As I was escorted out of the courtroom I looked for my father again. His seat was now empty. I assume that seeing me like that was just too much for him to handle.

I arrived back at the jailhouse with the same fanfare that greeted me when I left. People swore and spit at me. I was numb to it this time.

I was lost in my own head. My wife hadn't been there, my father had left, my mother was dead, my unborn child was dead. I was alone. There was no one there for me when I needed it.

I was led to a private cell. My overnight notoriety meant that it wasn't safe to keep me with other inmates, so I was kept isolated. I sat down on my bed and tried to make sense of everything.

Of course Sabrina wouldn't have come to my arraignment. It could have been interpreted as a show of support and she was obviously trying to distance herself from me in an effort to protect herself and her career.

Forever an optimist I began to concoct a story in my head for how Sabrina would come see me privately and explain everything. She'd apologize for what she had done and then explain why she had no choice but to do things the way she had. She'd share her master plan behind it all and how she was really working to get me out of this mess.

I heard footsteps approaching and the sound of keys jingling. My breath caught in my throat. I was certain that Sabrina had indeed come to visit me and soon all would be understood.

It *had* to be her coming to see me.

In a way I was correct.

"Inmate Yong, I have something for you," a guard said as he reached my cell.

I could see my name written on the envelope. It was Sabrina's handwriting. I took the letter from the guard and sat back down. Judging from the amount of paper in the envelope she had written me a long letter.

I eagerly removed the pages from the opened envelope and looked at the first one.

It wasn't a letter.

It was legal papers.

Sabrina had filed for divorce.

Chapter Ten

The Dream

"Daddy?"
"Daddy where are you?"

I'm here.

"I can't see you."

I can't see you either but I can hear you, son.

"I'm cold, Daddy."
"It's freezing here."

Follow my voice. Can you see my hand?

"I can't see anything."
"I'm so scared."

Reach out for my hand.

"Why did you put me here?"

"Why didn't you want me, Daddy?"
"Why didn't you love me?"

I do love you! Please… just take my hand! I love you more than anything! You're all I ever wanted!

"Then why didn't you let me live?"

Son… no… it wasn't me! It wasn't my fault! I didn't know!

"You let me die, Daddy."
"Why did you let Mommy kill me?"

NO! THAT'S NOT TRUE! I DIDN'T KNOW! PLEASE! JUST REACH FOR MY HAND! I'M HERE!

"You let me die, Daddy."

"You killed me, Daddy."

"... Daddy."

*"... **Daaaaaddyyyyyyy**..."*

Chapter Eleven

The Trial

My criminal trial began on October 3rd, 2007. "The People vs. Andrew Yong" was hailed as the "trial of *this* century." A very similar moniker had been used before, but the clocks had reset. Y2K came and went with nary a problem. Sure this was pretty early on in the grand scheme of the current century to throw that dubious accolade out, but as of today it still holds true. I don't think anything short of Bigfoot revealing himself and being brought to the Supreme Court will top it.

I was able to get a really great lawyer named Michael Manahan. I wish I could say that he took my case solely because of my obvious innocence. I wish I could say that he saw a great injustice happening and answered the call for righteousness.

The truth is that Manahan came to me because of the notoriety of the case. He knew what the national exposure would do for him. I don't fault him for that. He's gone on to become one of the most famous criminal defense lawyers in the nation. He was able to move on from all of this and live a full, wonderful life. That's a luxury that's always been out of my reach.

Manahan's entire defense was going to be the prosecution's lack of evidence. Plain and simple.

I was initially worried about my fingerprints being found on the belt-sander I used to fight off Victor Crowley but it came back clean. My fingerprints would not be found on any of the weapons that were uncovered at the crime scene.

Oddly, no fingerprints were found on *any* of the murder weapons. I saw Victor Crowley with my own two eyes and he was certainly not wearing gloves, which leads me to believe that his many deformities must have left him with no fingerprints at all.

Other than the fact that I was at the scene and the only survivor of the massacre, nothing tied me directly to a single crime. No motive, no murder weapon, no witness… no case.

Also, some of the remains found by the forensics team dated all the way back to the 1960's.

The bodies that didn't fit the Honey Island Swamp Massacre timeline were ultimately said to have been victims of another madman and not used against me in my trial. During my defense Manahan would be quick to point out the fact that the Honey Island Swamp killing field dated far back before I was even born. It only helped our case that I was not possibly responsible for whatever terrors were going on out there.

Louisiana had certainly been home to an unusually large amount of horrendous violence over the years. There has been no shortage of brutality in the bayou.

Emotionally I was a mess heading into the trial. I couldn't think straight and that's scary when you are locked in a cage at night with nothing but your thoughts.

I'm not into conspiracy theories. I think in many cases it dumbs us down as a society. I'm all for a search for truth. Once you discover the truth that should be it, but it never is for the nuts. They ignore the truth because everything has to have ulterior motives and a broader conspiracy at play.

In my case though, there definitely seemed to be something greater working against me. All info on the mystery girl was gone. My original statement from the night I was rescued had been lost. It all just seemed like too much of a coincidence.

Normally in a murder case the defendant does not take the stand under any circumstances. While there have of course been exceptions, a defendant on trial for murder typically stays off the stand. It is far too risky.

However, in my case I did not have a single alibi. I did not even have any character witnesses as everyone who knew me well had run for the hills or perished in the swamp. We may have had an arsenal of medical examiners and coroners to prove that there was no physical way that I could have possibly committed these atrociously brutal murders but someone had to appeal to the jury's humanity. As much as a trial should be based on the facts and only the facts, at the end of the day you're still talking about twelve human beings who are going to debate and come to a conclusion on a defendant's innocence or guilt. They were going to decide on a fellow human being's right to life or their imminent death.

After our front line of medical jargon I was literally all we had. I was prepared though. I wasn't hiding anything. I believed with all of my heart that if I got up there the jury would be able to see the real me. They would understand I wasn't possibly capable of doing harm to anyone.

Manahan and I had planned our strategy. The one thing that he was adamant about was that I do not mention Victor Crowley while I was on the stand. I would merely say that I did not know who did it. I never got a good look. It was dark.

All that mattered in winning my case was that I was proven to *not* have been the one who did it. We rehearsed over and over again until he was comfortable with how I would answer every possible question they could throw at me.

When it came time for me to take the stand I would be ready.

The prosecution spent three weeks calling their experts to the stand. They would attempt to explain how the victims had been killed in order to try to build anger in the jury. The details presented were horrific and there were many times when family members of the victims had to rush out of the courtroom.

What happened in the swamp was so sick, so obscene, that not even the autopsy photos could properly do it justice.

The prosecution was counting on the jurors getting bloodthirsty. They wanted an emotional reaction.

The exact opposite of what should happen in a fair trial.

Manahan was able to argue away every "fact" they presented. It was like a sporting event. The prosecution would serve him up evidence and he would effortlessly bat it right out of the courtroom with basic logic. While fleeting moments of doubt may have crept into my head in the weeks leading up to the trial, I was now feeling very confident that I would soon be acquitted.

The trial was rounding the corner towards the finish line and it was looking as though the prosecution would be resting their case without having been able to prove a single thing.

It was at this point that they turned their spotlight away from the swamp and instead shined it somewhere else.

My home.

Sabrina took the stand.

We had always known it was a possibility. She was on the prosecution's list of potential witnesses and after her grandiose self-preservation media stunt on the night I was arrested, we had suspected they would put her on the stand in the home stretch.

Manahan thought it was just a desperate, amateur hour tactic to try and rattle me.

Whether we considered the move to be a low blow by the prosecution or not, it succeeded in unraveling me. Sabrina was my kryptonite.

As she walked up to the stand I was overcome with emotion. I did my best to hold back my tears.

Manahan wasn't concerned about what Sabrina would say. I had assured him that there were no buried secrets there. I am who I am. I have always been an open book and I have always worn my heart on my sleeve.

Sabrina took the stand and swore in. I couldn't help but be captivated by her beauty all over again.

The prosecution began asking her how we met and she answered honestly. She told the story more or less how I always have. There was no hate in her voice and no fear. She was engaging and I felt like she was only succeeding in giving the jurors a sense of the man I really am.

I was wrong of course.

What the prosecution was really doing was endearing *Sabrina* to the jury by painting her as a loving and caring wife. Through all of this she never looked at me once. Based on her words and her demeanor I once again felt reassured that there was indeed still hope for us.

Finally, the prosecution asked her to look at me. I was going to get what I wanted. I was afraid to blink. I needed this connection. This is what I had been waiting for.

We looked into each other's eyes. She held the gaze for a moment before she looked away, a single tear streaming down her face.

"How would you describe Andrew's behavior during your marriage?" The prosecution asked.

She took a moment to center herself.

"Andrew has always had a vivid imagination. It's one of the reasons I fell in love with him. He has a very creative mind. But occasionally he blurred the lines between fiction and reality. He was prone to go on these tangents out of nowhere. He talked about fantastical things that couldn't be real. Sometimes the pictures on the walls would talk to him. I always considered it to be one of his many quirks.

He listened to a lot of heavy metal music, very blasphemous in nature. The album covers were filled with satanic imagery. It was ungodly and an insult to our Lord and Savior Jesus Christ. I tried not to judge him for the music he was into though. It was just his thing.

Sometimes when he would go to concerts he would paint his face in demonic shades of black and white. I was scared when I saw him like that but I didn't say anything.

Andrew had his own heavy metal band that he played with. *Haddonfield*. It's the name of the town in the horror movie where a killer in a white mask slashes up a bunch of young women."

"Have you ever seen Andrew become violent?" The prosecution asked.

"Despite all of the frightening things he was obsessed with, Andrew had always treated me well and he had never raised a hand to me.

Until the day that changed."

"Can you describe what happened that day?" The prosecution asked.

"He didn't hit me. But he wanted to. Instead, he punched a large hole in the wall of our house. It was the first time I saw him react violently.

They say the first hit is difficult for an abuser. But once that's out of the way it gets easier and easier. I was fearful of him after that."

I couldn't believe what I was hearing!
What was she doing?
This was airing to a nationwide audience!

Many people say that Sabrina's performance on the stand is what moved her into the upper echelon of the talk show ranks. It was certainly her big moment. She made it so.

The demonic way I'd paint my face? It goes without saying that I was a member of the *KISS* Army. Talking to pictures? Well, if she meant singing lyrics to posters of my favorite bands while I was jamming out… then sure.

Throwing me under the bus for the name of my band? As I've already stated, I've never even seen the movie *Halloween* and the band was called *Haddonfield* before I ever joined.

The coup de gras was her story about me punching a hole in the wall in an attempt to prove that I was prone to violence.

Yes, I punched a hole in the wall.

But it wasn't because I was upset. When it happened I didn't even know Sabrina was there. We were remodeling a room in the house. I needed to knock a wall down and I did. It just so happens I had watched a *Karate Kid* marathon that morning. I'm talking about part one and two. The movies after that are fun, but the first two are perfect. I wish they would have continued on with that story. Who knows… maybe someday?

I needed to knock down a wall and I was doing it with a sledgehammer. I struggled to swing it and almost fell down the first time. It was embarrassing and I was just glad no one was there to see it. Now I only wish people *had* seen it happen. It would make her accusations against me even more idiotic.

Some sections of the wall were easier to take down by hand. I would pull the sheetrock off of the studs. While doing that I had a *Karate Kid* "Miyagi moment." I gave a loud "hi-ya" and punched into the wall I was removing. My hand would hurt for a few days but not as much as my ego.

I had heard the laughter behind me and turned around quickly. Sabrina stood there grinning. I was embarrassed as hell but I did my best to laugh it off with her. She shook her head and walked away.

The way Sabrina presented these situations in court has affected me to this day. I'm in no way a violent person. I hate violence and I have thought that fighting was dumb ego jock stuff ever since getting bullied in grade school.

But to a nationwide audience, I was now painted as a crazy Satan worshiping man prone to outbursts of violence. Sabrina knew the truth. She knew that wasn't me. But she ran with it and many actually believed her. They still believe her.

"Where was Andrew the two nights before he was called out to Honey Island Swamp for work?" The prosecution asked.

"I don't know," she replied. "We had a very heated personal disagreement and he stormed out of the house. I stayed up late, hoping he would come home or call but he never did."

"Why didn't you call him?" They asked.

"Andrew's mother had just passed away earlier that week. The funeral was the day before. He was already very upset and not himself. Then we had our personal disagreement and… I was afraid of what he would do if I made him even more angry."

"What was the personal disagreement about?"

Sabrina took a deep breath for dramatic effect.

"Andrew had been trying to pressure me into having children with him. I told him I didn't think it was safe for him to be around a child with the way he acted."

It took everything I had to not scream. In fact, I don't know if I've ever been so angry in my life.

"So it's safe to say that you have no account of where he went for those two days then?"

"I do not know where he was."

During cross-examination, my lawyer was able to submit the credit card receipt for my hotel stay. It proved I had checked in.

I had spent the two nights writing and when you are lost in the creative process, time has a way of slipping away. It did for me.

I never left my room, not even to eat. I never ordered room service. I had no luggage with me. When Jim called me in to work I left in such a rush that I forgot to check out. This is usually not a problem. Hotels automatically check you out if you forget to. When housekeeping went into my room to clean it they found that the bed was still made and it appeared like no one had been there. I was there though, I assure you. I worked diligently on the song I was writing for Sabrina and then I had passed out on top of the blankets.

This unfortunately meant that no one at the hotel could vouch that I was actually there.

"Tell me about March 13th, 2007," the prosecution asked.

"A detective came to the studio to talk to me," Sabrina said.

"You were working?" The prosecution asked.

"Yes. After the death of Andrew's Mom, God rest her soul, Andrew had been unable to work. He was too emotionally distraught and unstable. I had tried to console him and offer support but all he wanted to do was lie in the bedroom with the shades pulled down and be left alone. I wanted to give him some space and since we had just put a substantial amount of money into the funeral I needed to keep working."

"What did the detective want to talk to you about?" The prosecution asked.

"Andrew," she replied. "They informed me that they were going to arrest him and that they needed my help in having it go as smoothly as possible. They didn't want anyone to get hurt."

"What did they want you to do?" He asked.

"Make sure he was calm and relaxed," she answered.

"Tell me what happened when you arrived at your home."

"Andrew was inebriated from the anti-anxiety medication he was prescribed," she replied. "He had been taking numerous different pills ever since he was released from the hospital. I walked into the house and he immediately came towards me in a threatening manner. He was in one of his moods. I tried to get him to calm down, but he wouldn't listen.

He had taken so many pills that day that he could no longer control himself. He smashed a lamp and picked up the letter opener."

They showed the jury the footage from the day I was arrested. You can hear me scream at Sabrina and then the door opens. I look unhinged. I was drugged up, distraught and yes angry.

Of course, I wasn't in control of my emotions. My marriage was collapsing, I had just buried my mother, my wife had terminated our unborn baby and I had survived the most horrific massacre in the history of the United States.

I still don't know why I didn't bring up the abortion during the trial. I think it was still too personal for me. I never even told my lawyers. I now wish I had told everyone.

Maybe it would have caused Sabrina to look less perfect than the role she was currently portraying.

Maybe it would have made me look like less of the monster she was turning me into.

Sabrina was on the stand for almost six hours. It's the longest stretch of time I've been with her since my arrest.

Only towards her last few minutes on the stand did it finally dawn on me.

My ex-wife was trying to kill me.

I was facing the death penalty if I was found guilty.

I knew at that moment that she truly believed I had done this.

The prosecution rested and it was now time to present our case.

For the first few days of our defense we had various medical experts take the stand. We also called on several of the coroners that had personally handled the victim's remains.

One by one Manahan meticulously brought them through every victim recovered in Honey Island Swamp and proved again and again that no human being, especially not a man of my size and stature, could have possibly committed the atrocious and brutal physical feats of strength.

Of course the prosecution tried everything they could to cast doubt on our medical experts. In their cross-examinations they proposed hypothetical questions about the abnormal effects that the various medications I was on could have possibly had on my mind and body.

Our witnesses held firm.

As concrete as their testimony may have been in my defense, we were still worried. The medical and technical information could easily get lost in translation on a jury of random men and women.

Sabrina had all but assassinated my character and we needed to offer a human counterpoint to show the jurors who I really was.

It was finally time for me to take the stand.

Manahan and I went through our questions exactly as rehearsed. As expected, the prosecution tried their hardest to cast doubt on my answers. They tried to get me to stumble on the facts as I knew them.

As I went back and forth being interrogated by Manahan and the prosecution I covered my upbringing and what had led me to choose the vocation I had.

I discussed the passion and joy I felt in helping people. I mentioned my impeccable service record as an EMT. I praised my co-workers, referring to them more as friends and family. I reminded everyone that I too had lost many people in that swamp. I was positive the jury felt my true sorrow over their loss.

It was hard, but I even spoke of my undying love for Sabrina. I made sure that everyone knew that I was in a hotel writing my wife a song through the first two nights of the massacre. I explained what had really happened with me punching a hole in the wall. I let it be known that in testifying against me I knew Sabrina was only doing what she thought she needed to do to protect her precious career.

I made sure that both she and the jury heard loud and clear that I forgave her for everything she had previously embellished in her attempt to distance herself from me.

As planned, we saved Manahan's final question until after the prosecution had announced that they had no further questions. Once they conceded Manahan would ask me "who did it?" and I would answer, "I don't know, but it was not me."

I looked at the jurors and I could see that they were struggling to believe that I had possibly committed the crimes. As we approached the finish line I felt the oppressive weight of the last seven months begin to lift off of my shoulders.

I was almost home free.

The lead prosecutor approached the stand and showed me pictures of two of the victims.

"Do you recognize these two men, Mr. Yong?" He asked.

I looked at the photos.

Both of the men were Chinese. They both appeared to be around my same age give or take a year or two. They both looked like me.

They looked *a lot* like me.

Randy's voice echoed in my head…

"Crazy shit. I was just working on an Asian male that has his head cut off and his leg missing below the knee. He actually looks like you."

The fact still remained that I had never seen either man before in my life.

I answered that I did not recognize the men.

"Look again, Mr. Yong," he said. "This man's name was Shawn. This man's name was Justin. They were brothers. Are you *sure* you don't recognize them?"

"No. I do not know them," I answered.

I couldn't figure out where the prosecution was possibly going with this line of questioning.

"You're absolutely positive that you've never even *seen* these men before Mr. Yong?"

I looked at the pictures again and answered honestly.

"Beyond a shadow of a doubt."

"Then can you explain why *your* DNA was discovered on *both* of their bodies?"

The courtroom collectively gasped.

"Objection!" Manahan quickly shouted and stood up. "We were not provided with any of this supposed evidence!"

"We only just received this evidence, Your Honor," the prosecution replied.

The Judge called both lawyers to the bench and began a hushed conversation. I was unable to hear what was being said, but I could tell that Manahan was incredibly upset.

The quiet chatting that had slowly started in the crowd of courtroom watchers intensified in volume until there were actual shouts coming from some of the victims' families.

"They've got that bastard dead to rights!" I heard one spectator's voice declare.

The Judge called a recess to give the heated commotion time to settle down.

During the recess Manahan was livid. It was the first time I saw him truly panic.

"Can they do that?" I asked him. "I thought it was required for all evidence to be shared during the discovery process?"

"Of course they can't do that," Manahan replied. "The Judge will certainly throw it out."

"Then what's the problem?" I asked.

"The jury already heard it," Manahan said, defeated. "The whole fucking world just heard it. It's probably already on the news!"

My stomach slowly began to sink.

This was very, very bad.

"It all makes sense now," Manahan said. "This is why it took them a full week to bring charges against you in the first place. They were looking for something – *anything* - to bring you down with. This is bad for us, Andrew. This is very, very bad."

My head spun with the realization that I may be given a lethal injection after all. I was going to be put to death for crimes that I absolutely did not commit.

"Is there something you want to tell me about that DNA?" Manahan asked me.

"Of course not!" I retorted. "I have no idea what they're even talking about!"

Manahan paced the small holding room we were in. He began ringing his hands. His defeated behavior scared the hell out of me.

I should mention that by now my case had become more than just exposure for Manahan. He knew I was innocent. There was absolutely no molecule in his body that debated that fact.

However, I should also stress again that he did not in any way believe that Victor Crowley was real. It's why he had forbidden me from bringing up Crowley on the stand. He said my story would make me look like I was mentally ill. While that would have definitely worked had we been going for a plea of insanity, that was obviously not the position we were taking. I was innocent and therefore the prosecution's sheer lack of evidence was supposed to have been enough to clear me of these preposterous allegations.

Still, I had argued with him early on that as crazy as my story sounded it was indeed the truth. Now with a supposed DNA match on two of the victims I asked Manahan once again if I should tell the court what really happened with Victor Crowley. I was worried.

He didn't care. He wanted to stick to the facts, the lack of evidence, and not succumb to conjecture.

There was a knock at the door and a bailiff handed Manahan a sheet of paper.

"What is it?" I asked.

"The DNA evidence," Manahan replied as he began to read the information. It only took a few seconds for him to begin smirking. "This is bullshit. It proves nothing. The DNA is highly consistent with yours, I'll give them that, but the percentage isn't high enough to be an indisputable match. If it had been they never would have risked letting this get thrown out. They would have submitted it properly right up front. They only brought this up here at the end to damage you in the court of public opinion."

He put his hands on both of my shoulders.

"Do you get it?" He said. "This isn't even about *you* at this point. They know they're going to lose! This DNA bullshit was simply a Hail Mary for the State to try and save face.

They want the world to think that they did their job.

When you get exonerated, they'll make an announcement saying that they are no longer investigating the crimes as a way of saying to the public that they *did* solve the case and bring the villain down. Justice failed, not *them*. Those dirty bastards."

What Manahan was saying made sense to me. It was almost identical to the O.J. Simpson trial. When O.J. walked free the prosecution said that they weren't going to keep looking for the killer. It was their way of saying "we already showed you the killer but <u>you</u> let him go."

The only difference here was that I was not a killer.

Manahan sternly instructed me to steer the course and to not let their cheap shots and desperate antics shake me. My only job was to keep saying, "I didn't do it" as they couldn't prove otherwise no matter what they threw at me.

All I had to do now was stick to the same plan that had already carried us to the final round of the fight.

I'd be going home soon.

We were called back into court and as Manahan had expected, the Judge immediately dismissed the surprise DNA “evidence” as inadmissible to the court and ordered the jurors to disregard it.

But the prosecution had expertly staged this maneuver and the fact that my DNA was *supposedly* found on two of the bodies was all anyone talked about from that point forward.

It was the moment where I was permanently crucified by the world. DNA evidence is the cornerstone of most cases. It’s the smoking gun. To this day that suggested and discarded DNA plagues me. It wasn’t even a full match yet it is what the public at large clings to in their claim that I am in fact guilty despite my proven innocence. It is the scarlet letter that I will wear for the rest of my life.

With court back in session the prosecution resumed his cross-examination of me.

“Who is Victor Crowley?” He asked.

Once again I was caught completely off guard. I looked at Manahan and could see his eyes piercing through me, warning me. I kept my cool and stuck to our plan.

"Victor Crowley," I said, "he's a local legend used to scare kids."

I wasn't lying. This was the truth.

"So he's not the one responsible for all of these murders then?" The prosecution asked.

"Objection!" Manahan stood and stated.

"Overruled", the Judge responded. He turned back to the prosecution. "Counselor, I'll give you thirty seconds to show me where you're going with this."

"Of course, Your Honor," he replied. "I'll ask you again, Mr. Yong. Is Victor Crowley the one who murdered all of these innocent people?"

I ran all the scenarios through my head. How could I respond to this?

"OBJECTION!" Manahan shouted.

"Sustained," the Judge said. "Let's wrap this up, Counselor."

"Mr. Yong, are you responsible for the murders?" The prosecution asked.

"No," I replied.

"Then who is? A legend? A ghost?"

He took a long pause between each sentence as he looked around the courtroom. Letting it all hang there. He smiled at me.

All I had to do was say “I don’t know.” It was that simple. Just say “I don’t know” and this would all be over. I looked towards Manahan for some guidance. His eyes pleaded with me to say what he had rehearsed me to say.

But I was confused.

My original statement to the police on the night I was rescued had mysteriously been lost along with any information that the Jefferson Parish Police Department had on the identity of “Jane Doe.” Where did the prosecution possibly get this information about me having watched Victor Crowley kill everyone?

I looked at Sabrina sitting a few rows behind the prosecution. My heart stopped in my chest as we stared into each other’s eyes.

She smirked. I knew the look well. It was a condescending “fuck you” smirk that told me all I needed to know.

She had told the prosecution everything.

I raged inside.

"Answer the question, Mr. Yong," the Judge said.

"Victor Crowley is responsible for the murders," I answered.

"OBJECTION!" Manahan screamed as he rose to his feet.

"Overruled!" The Judge replied.

The crowd in the courtroom exploded with a mixture of shouts, anger, and laughter.

"Order!" The Judge yelled as he slammed his gavel down repeatedly. "Order in the court!"

There was no turning back now. The world was going to know who had really done all of this.

For the next several minutes the truth cascaded from my lips. I told them how Victor Crowley had torn everyone apart single-handedly. Guns didn't stop him. A bazooka didn't stop him. I did everything I could but in the end it was a miracle that I had survived.

It came out fast and furiously.

I told them *everything*.

By the end I was crying.

The response was complete silence. No one spoke.

I looked at the Judge and he stared at me with his mouth agape.

I looked at Manahan. He held his head in his hands.

I looked at the crowd in their seats. Everyone seemed to be in shock.

I looked at the prosecution. He grinned from ear to ear. "No further questions, Your Honor."

I looked at Sabrina, tears streaming down my face. She shook her head and scoffed in disgust.

It started slowly at first.

I could hear quiet murmuring and then the anger poured out in full force. Once again the audience that had gathered to watch began yelling. Some people even cackled as though I was on stage at a comedy club and had just delivered a knock out punchline.

Once again the Judge began to bang his gavel and ask for order in the court.

This time it didn't work.

I was escorted back into the holding room while the bailiff and other court security officers' worked to regain order over the commotion out in the courtroom.

My thoughts turned back to the night of my rescue. My original statement that had gone missing along with any of the details about "Jane Doe."

Obviously someone powerful wanted to keep the truth silent. They had done everything they could to ensure that I would be the one to go down for everything. *But why?*

I have theories but I'll likely never know the truth.

Victor Crowley had always been a local ghost story. My trial changed that. This was the very first time his name was so much as uttered on the world's stage. These days everyone knows who he is.

"Do you realize what the hell you have done?" Manahan said, closing the door behind him as he stepped into the room.

"I told the truth," I replied.

"You've fucked yourself. What was the one mantra we kept repeating?" He said as he paced around the room.

"No Victor Crowley", I muttered.

He stared back at me. "The lack of evidence sets you free. Not the truth."

Looking back, I don't regret it for one moment. It was my experience. It was real. It was the truth. It *is* the truth. It really happened.

Once I mentioned Victor Crowley the trial became a spectacle. Viewership skyrocketed. Within six months a whole commercial industry would pop up because of my testimony on the stand. Many have now profited from the Honey Island Massacre.

For most, my testimony only reinforced their belief that I was the killer but Manahan was only concerned with the twelve people in the jury box. Luckily they had been sequestered so they weren't subjected to all of the nonsense permeating the airwaves. His fear was that they would lose focus on the evidence or in this case the lack of, and that they would grasp onto the "*pure madness Andrew Yong vomited all over the courtroom.*"

The public's words, not mine.

We were brought back into the courtroom and the trial continued, though I would never take the stand again.

Manahan was a cunning attorney and therefore he already had a back-up plan ready to go should an emergency blindside him in the trial.

He just hadn't expected the emergency to come from his own client.

Regardless, he still had a card to play.

He called two separate doctors to the stand in order to attest to the fact that I was suffering from a medical condition that could hinder my ability to properly process what I had experienced.

Post-traumatic stress disorder, PTSD for short, is defined as: *a condition of persistent mental and emotional stress occurring as a result of injury or severe psychological shock, typically involving disturbance of sleep and constant vivid recall of the experience, with dulled responses to others and to the outside world.*

There was no doubt I had PTSD. How could you survive a situation like mine and not? Both doctors said that my recollection is almost a textbook example of the condition.

The information seemed to sit well with the court. It wasn't going to do anything to prove that I hadn't killed everyone but Manahan's goal at that point was merely to put a Band-Aid on any bruises to my character that my Victor Crowley breakdown may have left the jury with.

PTSD or not, I didn't imagine what I went through though.

Victor Crowley is real.

It's true that the remains of Victor Crowley were never located. Not a trace. From what I could surmise it sounded like the alligators got him, but without a body as evidence we'll never know for sure.

I expected him to come back to life the next night, just as I had seen him do during my long night in the swamp. But Victor Crowley did not return that next night.

In fact, to this day he has never reappeared again.

The prosecution's closing arguments centered almost entirely on my tale of Victor Crowley. They repeated my testimony about him verbatim while showing the jurors more photos of the many people that had perished in the swamp. It was an astute tactic but it was also all they had.

Manahan stuck to the lack of evidence for the majority of his remarks. He then held up a picture of me.

"Many people lost their lives and that is a terrible tragedy. I was certainly moved by the pictures the prosecution showed you. They are the innocent victims in all this. But so is Andrew Yong. We can't lose perspective on that.

The prosecution has shown you that there is absolutely no evidence indicting Andrew Yong. You are all smart. You clearly see that. The forensic and medical experts proved to you that Andrew Yong could not physically have been responsible for those deaths. You clearly see that, too.

I know we want answers. We want to punish someone. We want justice for those that were taken from us in such horrendous and despicable ways. Someone is accountable. But it is not Andrew. He does not deserve blame here. He went through an experience that most could not have survived. He persevered at a great cost.

We've had two doctors take the stand to discuss Andrew's PTSD. That is real. That is documented. This trial isn't about his recollection of events. It can't be. It has to be about the *evidence*. Of which there is none.

I'm holding up Andrew's picture because it belongs with those that the prosecution showed you. Andrew is most certainly a victim as well. You do not have to believe his testimony in order to come back with a not guilty verdict. You just have to believe the *facts* of the case… the *evidence*. And I know you will."

The jury took three days to return a verdict. I expected it to come back much sooner. I thought they might walk out of the courtroom, turn around and come right back in. But that didn't happen.

With each day they deliberated my faith plummeted.

By the third day I was sure I'd be found guilty and so was Manahan. He was already preparing the appeals.

I wanted to go into the deliberation room, talk to the people on the jury, and find out what they were thinking.

I've now had the opportunity to do so. Not personally, but through their own written words. Most of them have books out.

I've read them all.

Victor Crowley was the hang up for most. It was the moment where they began to wonder. And they should wonder. We should all wonder. If Victor Crowley is real, and he is… what *else* is out there?

They returned a verdict at the very end of the third day.

Not Guilty.

I want to repeat that.

Not Guilty.

After a grueling six week trial "The People vs. Andrew Yong" was finally over.

I was found 'not guilty' by a jury of my peers.

I was released from custody later that same day.

I thought that would be the end of my ordeal.

I thought that I would finally be able to get back to my life.

I thought wrong.

Chapter Twelve

The Aftermath

Manahan had given me strict instruction not to show any signs of happiness in the event that I was found innocent when the verdict was read. Most of the world would be watching my face in extreme close-up as the debacle came to an end and the major news outlets would certainly replay and analyze my reaction for days to come after the verdict.

While I may have been overjoyed to be walking away from the nightmare alive and cleared of the crimes I did not commit, in the end at least forty people were still dead. Their families and loved ones were forever torn apart by what Victor Crowley had done to them.

I had personally lost about 75% of the friends that I worked with every day, though no one on the outside ever seemed to consider or empathize with all that I had personally lived through and lost. To the world, I was still the boogeyman and I was still guilty even if proven innocent.

Needless to say, when you're convinced that you're going to be wrongfully put to death by lethal injection and then you suddenly find yourself a free man and cleared of all charges… you can't help but be happy and grateful to be going home alive.

Unfortunately, home had changed entirely in the long time I had been away. I barely recognized my house when I finally walked inside. Sabrina had long since moved out and taken just about everything with her. I was grateful that my divorce attorney had seen to it that she could not sell our house until there was a verdict in my trial and that I had a home to return to upon release, but walking into an empty shell of what had once been my life was a shocking dose of reality for me.

All that was left were a few mismatched dishes in the cabinets, a few piles of my clothes on the floor of the guest room, one wobbly nightstand, my record collection, and a pile of photo albums in the master bedroom. Stacked neatly beneath our two wedding albums were the framed pictures of Sabrina and I that had once decorated our home.

Beneath those was the engagement ring I had proposed to Sabrina with. It would have hurt less if she had pawned it.

For all of the nights I had dreamed of sleeping in my own bed again… my bed was gone. I would wind up sleeping on the floor for the next several weeks and using my clothes as pillows and blankets.

As lonely as prison had been, being on the outside again was even lonelier. At least in prison there were regular visits from Manahan and I had guards to speak to. At home there was nothing. When I was on trial I would often think about the news footage of O.J. Simpson returning home to a house full of friends and family that were waiting to celebrate his return. The way I saw it, if a guy who was clearly guilty could receive that kind of homecoming, my homecoming would be even greater.

In jail, I had often fantasized about coming home to a long receiving line of family, friends, and co-workers all apologizing for not standing by me through the entire ordeal. One by one they would admit that they were wrong to doubt my innocence and ask what they can possibly do to make it up to me. At the very end of the line would be Sabrina who would literally fall to her knees and beg for my forgiveness with tears streaming down her face. My ex-wife would plead with me to take her back and after attending a few marriage counseling sessions together eventually I would.

But no one came to see me.

No one even called.

You can only imagine my humiliation when I called the phone company just to check if my phone line was indeed still active.

"You're calling us on your home phone line, Mr. Yong. Clearly, it's still working."

I convinced myself that Sabrina just needed a few days before she would be ready to swallow her pride, come home, and apologize. But where were the other guys from *Haddonfield*? Where were my co-workers that were still alive? Wouldn't whoever was now running the station want to know when I was coming in to work again?

Where was my father?

At the request of my neighbors, the police did not allow any crowds to gather in front of my home on the day I was released. Instead, a small handful of protesters had gathered down the street holding various signs declaring me a murderer and letting me know that I would someday rot in hell.

If they only knew that I had already survived hell perhaps they would have come up with something more creative for their ridiculous signs.

The protests only lasted a few days, with the crowd diminishing by half each morning. On the second day, I walked down to the protest line to speak to the police who were keeping the crowd from storming down my street with their virtual pitchforks and torches. I only got about halfway there before the officer in charge cut me off at the pass.

"I'm going to need to ask that you remain inside," the officer said. "We don't want to aggravate the crowd and have a confrontation."

I obliged but I asked him to please let through any friends or family that were trying to come see me.

"No one has come to see you yet but we'll let you know if that happens."

It never happened.

I had essentially traded one jail cell for another. I was too scared of what might happen if I dared go out in public. By my fourth day at home, I was going crazy pacing the empty rooms of my house. Like a scene out of *Robocop*, I kept seeing my home as it was before the night that would ultimately destroy my life. I'd walk into a room and it would appear bright and happy at first but then fade back into the dark and dusty empty cell it had become. Sometimes my mind would play tricks on me and I'd hear Sabrina in the shower or imagine her sleeping next to me only to reach out and get a handful of empty floor.

Without a television to watch or a radio to listen to I could only imagine what was being said about me in the media. To try and get my mind off of it I would read every piece of junk mail I received over and over again. I studied every flier from the local supermarket, often times memorizing what was on sale. It wasn't only my fear of the outside world that kept me from going food shopping.

Sabrina had taken the refrigerator.

I had pizza delivered every second day and I would make it last for two breakfasts, two lunches, and two dinners.

In an effort to disguise my face, I began growing out my facial hair. I figured that once I had cultivated a nice, thick beard it would be safe to attempt going out in public. Some nights I would find myself staring into the bathroom mirror and literally watching my hair (not) grow. Sadly, even in my 30's, I still couldn't grow a decent beard.

By the end of my first week at home, I began to receive some letters in the mail. Here are a few examples:

Andrew-

Her name was Avery and she was my daughter. I've enclosed a photograph of her so that you won't be able to forget her face and what you did to her. For reasons that I'll never understand, you decided to take her from my family. To the best of my knowledge, you didn't even know Avery and she just happened to be in the wrong place at the wrong time. Therefore, it is important to me that you know just who the sweet and innocent woman was that you sadistically murdered.

Avery was an extremely happy baby. She was singing before she learned how to speak. She played softball in High School and she was "Anna" in her school's production of The King And I. When she was 17 she selflessly donated all of her Christmas gifts to charity. She sacrificed going to college in order to immediately go to work for the Salvation Army after High School and do everything that she could to help others. Avery spent her last three Thanksgivings on this earth volunteering at a homeless shelter in downtown New Orleans. She was a virgin and had always promised her mother and I that she would wait until she was married before she would lay with a man. She was a perfect, God loving Christian girl. She was my angel.

According to the police report, Avery's clothes had been torn from her body prior to you striking her directly between her breasts with your hatchet blade and ending her life. My wife and I fear that you may have raped our daughter before murdering her but we'll never know for sure, will we? Apparently, you also struck her in between the legs with that blade and mutilated her genitals in order to hide any evidence of what you really did to her. I've tried to imagine the fear and the pain that you inflicted upon her during her final moments but my mind is incapable of imagining such evil thoughts.

Our pastor has told my wife and I numerous times that we need to make peace with Avery's passing and find it in our hearts to forgive you for the unbearable pain and suffering that you have caused us. But we cannot forgive you and we never will. If that means that my wife and I will be denied seeing our daughter again in heaven then so be it. We will see you in hell, Andrew.

I have thought long and hard about how I would kill you but I have decided against it. While I would gladly go to prison for the rest of my life, killing you would be letting you off too easy for what you did to Avery. Instead I will continue to get on my knees every single night and pray that someday you lose a child in the same vicious manner that we have. I want your child to be taken from you in the most horrific way possible. I want your child to be raped and then slowly chopped into little pieces by a monster like yourself. I want you to lay awake at night hearing your child's screams of pain just like I will in my dreams for the rest of my life.

I hope that Avery's face haunts you for the rest of your days on earth.

I want you to remember her smile in the enclosed picture as you burn for all of eternity.

You may have beaten the legal system but you cannot defy God. When the day finally comes that you receive His judgment, He will not show mercy for your sins. If anything, you've only made your eventual suffering in hell worse by avoiding your due punishment here on earth. My family takes solace in that fact.

- *Avery's Daddy*

Murderer –

Not today.
Not tonight.
Not tomorrow.
But when you least expect it.
I am going to kill you for what you did.

Sleep with one eye open.

- *Anonymous*

Dear Mr. Yong –

I am a great admirer of your work. In the coming days I am going to shoot up a school near me and blame it on a ghost, too. You will know my name at that time.

You are my inspiration and I am your loyal servant. Every child's soul that I take is my gift to you.

- *Anonymous*

Andrew-

Forgive me for not reaching out sooner. As I hope you can understand, this experience has completely broken me. I am only grateful that your mother did not live to have to witness all of this.

Shortly after your trial began I was fired from work and then evicted from my condo by the Home Owners' Association just 30 days later. A friend was kind enough to take me in for a few weeks while I changed my name and found a new place to live far away from Louisiana.

I'm sorry that I never came to visit. I'm sorry that I never called. I'm sorry that I never wrote until now. I did not know what to think or what to do. To be honest, I still don't. How could my sweet son do those horrible things? It just doesn't make any sense.

I am relieved that the law has spared you and I pray that you will succeed in building a new life. Unfortunately, it will need to be a life without me in it. At least for now.

Forgive me, son. I need time to process all of this and get my own life back to some semblance of normal before I can even think about beginning the long healing process that we will need to go through together after this terrible ordeal. For now, I need to keep my head down and forge a new path under my new name and identity. I will find you when I am ready to reconnect.

- *Dad*

Last year a distant cousin in China that I have never met emailed me to let me know that my father had passed away. Apparently, my Dad had been living with extended family just outside of Shenzhen for the past decade. He died from heart failure, which naturally makes me blame myself. Had I only not answered my phone that day or had I just been killed in that swamp along with everyone else perhaps my father's heart wouldn't have suffered the way it did for the last decade of his life. I believe that he is reunited with my mother now.

By the end of my first week as a free man, I was starting to fear that Sabrina was never going to reach out to me, let alone come home.

It may seem crazy that I even wanted to see Sabrina again, let alone repair our relationship and try again. In the days that followed my release I thought long and hard about why she had turned her back on me. I was able to rationalize just why she had testified against me so venomously. I had been facing the death penalty and she seemed to have done whatever she could do to help ensure that happened.

I knew that her initial actions of publicly cooperating with the authorities and televising it to the world were merely an act of self-preservation. She knew that they were coming for me and nothing was going to change that. Her career was everything to her. She had worked so very hard to get to where she was and being associated with an alleged mass murderer would have destroyed all that she had accomplished. Standing by and blindly defending me would have been suicide for her.

But this wasn't just about Sabrina's career. I've since come to the conclusion that she truly believed I had done it. The lack of any evidence aside, the sheer circumstances of the situation certainly painted me as the only possible solution for the killer. Putting myself in her shoes I can only imagine that her mind was made up the moment that I told her about Victor Crowley. I wouldn't have believed me either.

Not to make excuses for my own wife having testified against me in a capital punishment trial but I have since learned that even if the jury had indeed found me guilty, I never would have actually been given the death penalty. Without a confession, a murder weapon, a motive, or a witness, the worst I would have received is a life in prison and many, many years of appeals. I choose to assume that she knew that before she ever agreed to aid the prosecution in hunting me down.

In my mind Sabrina was still my wife and I still loved her. I may not have owed her a chance at forgiveness but that didn't stop me from wanting so badly to give her one. I imagined that she was suffering under the weight of the mistakes she had made. Mistakes that were only human. After all, the entire world *still* thinks I did it. It's just easier to blame me than to accept the terrifying truth about what had happened in Honey Island Swamp. With how insane my story was I couldn't blame her for not just choosing to stand by me and watch her own life burn down around her just for doing so. She did what she needed to do and what she thought was right. She felt humiliated and betrayed that her husband had actually been a serial killer. She had felt that it was her duty to the families of the victims to do her part in making sure that justice was served.

Now that I had been cleared I was confident that she was devastated over all of it. I wanted to give her a chance to come home and start over again. I just needed to speak to her.

Unfortunately, there were two significant reasons why I couldn't just contact Sabrina myself. The first was that I had no idea where she was living or what her new phone number might be. The second, more complicated reason was that my legal team had explicitly warned me not to initiate contact with my ex-wife for fear that she might consider it harassment and slap me with a restraining order. I may have been exonerated but that didn't mean I wasn't still on thin ice with the authorities.

When you factor in just how many of the victims were law enforcement it's not hard to comprehend that every official with a badge would be looking for any reason they could find to harass me, arrest me, and put me back behind bars. All it would take is one call to the police from Sabrina claiming I was "stalking" her and I'd be back in jail again.

That might sound dramatic but given Sabrina's behavior, anything and everything was possible.

I was fast asleep on my laundry palette when I heard the front door open downstairs. The door had opened naturally and in my sleep, I thought I had heard the sound of keys so I was more excited than concerned. I wish I could say that my first instinct upon hearing someone enter my home was to find a weapon to protect myself with but in my heartbroken longing to see Sabrina again my first move was to race to the bathroom, splash some water on my face, and try and make myself as presentable as I possibly could.

I stepped out of the bathroom to find a man standing at the top of the stairs. He was wearing a ski mask and dressed all in black. I seemed to have startled him almost as much as he had surprised me and at first, we just stood there facing each other. He was a good twenty feet away from me but he was also blocking the stairs, which were my only escape.

It's incredible just how much can go through your head in a split second when you're beyond terrified. As my mind reeled I concocted a whole story in my mind that the intruder merely thought my house was abandoned and was breaking in to see what he may be able to steal. I was confident that he would start running once he processed that the only thing left in the house was the owner.

That's when he flashed the knife.

"Murderer," his deep, hoarse voice threatened.

Instinct kicked in and I leaped back inside the bathroom, which was thankfully the only room in the house with a lock on it. A second later the man began pounding relentlessly on the door, splintering the flimsy wood under the weight of his fists and feet.

I knew I didn't have much time before he would be inside the bathroom and plunging that knife deep into my chest. I pushed open the window, kicked out the screen, and slid myself outside where I jumped two stories into the bushes below.

I would realize much later that the fall had sprained my ankle and that I had cut up my legs on the branches, but my adrenaline was pumping. I managed to sprint across the street to my neighbor's house.

Thankfully my neighbor showed me some kindness and let me inside immediately. Together we watched my attacker race out of my front door and flee down the street.

I used my neighbor's phone to call the police.

"911 what is your emergency?"

"A man just broke into my home and attacked me with a knife!"

"Is the man still there, sir?"

"No, I'm across the street at my neighbor's. But he's running away now!"

"Are you still in danger?"

"I don't know! Send someone!"

"What is your location, Sir?"

"My address is ______________. Hurry! You can still catch him!""

TYPING NOISES.

"Your name, Sir?"

"Andrew Yong. Please, send someone quick!"

CLICK.

That night I learned that I was never going to be safe again. My house is burning down? The fire department isn't answering. Someone attacks me with a knife in my own home? The cops weren't coming.

Hell, for all I know the local police were behind the attack.

I knew that life would be very different for me. I just hadn't expected it to become the Wild West.

My fear of how the public may treat me had kept me from such basic things as food shopping or even just going for a walk in my own neighborhood. It would be another two months before I'd go shopping for new furniture, but the very next day I began the process of applying for a gun license.

It came as no surprise that my application was immediately denied.

I've applied for a license to carry a firearm once a year since 2008. My application has either been denied or "lost in the mail" every time.

I've since found other forms of legal self-defense to keep on me or within grabbing reach in my home at all times.

In fact, I still sleep with a little something special under my pillow to this day.

Early one morning I was contacted by Manahan's assistant who told me she had received multiple offers from PR firms looking to represent me for television appearances.

I signed with the first firm I spoke to.

Though I knew it would be a mistake to try and defend myself on television, at the end of the day I needed money desperately. My publicist advised that we create a bidding war for my first public appearance and see which show was willing to pony up the most cash.

I had delusions of grandeur that I would get at least six figures for five or ten minutes on television but out of the three talk shows that made offers the most I was offered was two hundred dollars and a cab to and from the studio.

No one else was biting.

While it may have been stupid of me to willingly put myself into such a volatile situation for two hundred bucks and a cab ride what I ultimately did was far stupider.

I told my publicist that I would only appear on one show and one show only.

"The Sabrina Show."

If my ex-wife wouldn't speak to me privately then I'd force her to have to speak to me publicly. If appearing on Sabrina's show was the only way to get a few minutes with her again then I would do it.

For free.

I knew that her producers would bite as what could possibly make for better ratings than a beloved talk show host interviewing her ex-husband who was now the most hated man in the country?

My plan worked and Sabrina's producers booked me immediately.

The interview was scheduled to take place exactly one week later. Though all talk shows are recorded in advance of their eventual broadcast, in an unprecedented move for "The Sabrina Show", the *special event* was to take place live and be a half-hour long. There would not be a live studio audience, only the cameras.

Sabrina's producers promoted the hell out of the special and advertised it as "*the interview of this century*." When I saw the commercials I should have known what I was in for as the advertisements were produced to look more like an upcoming boxing match than an interview.

I ran through the interview in my mind over and over again all week long trying to convince myself that I would not only be able to clear my name but also win my wife back.

If you saw the interview then you already know that I also had a trick up my sleeve.

It was a trick that would backfire on me in the most humiliating way possible.

When I arrived at the studio I was taken aback by how friendly everyone was to me. I'm not sure what I expected but given that the whole world seemed to hate me I was prepared for dirty looks from the staff and possibly even the usual "murderer" name calling I was becoming accustomed to.

Instead, the staff doted on me as if I was one of the typical Hollywood celebrities that they handled on a daily basis. There was a tremendous food spread in my dressing room and every few minutes a production assistant would ask me if I needed anything.

I paced back and forth in the dressing room waiting for Sabrina to come in and say hello to me before the interview like she always did for each guest. As the minutes clicked by I began to realize that she wasn't going to. When the assistant director knocked to have the make-up artist touch me up one last time I flat out asked for Sabrina.

"Sabrina apologizes but she is very busy, Mr. Yong. She'll see you out there," he said.

My heart sank. As fast as the make-up artist touched me up I sweat right through the inch or so of make-up it felt like she had already plastered on my worried face.

Finally, the knock came that was followed by the dreaded "we're ready for you, Mr. Yong."

As I walked down the backstage hallway towards the stage door I was brought right back to the feeling I had on the day my verdict was going to be read.

I felt like I was walking to my own execution.

When I took my seat on the interview couch I caught a glimpse of Sabrina on the other side of the stage. A full team of hair and make-up artists swarmed around her, blocking her face from me. I tried to relax with deep breaths as I waited for her to take her seat next to me. I almost felt like I had myself together when I noticed the screen behind me.

I began to panic.

Whoever was running the projector was cycling through the various images they would be showing behind us during the interview.

Every image was a photo of a different victim.

It was a trap and I had willingly set it for myself.

Sabrina finally took her seat as the assistant director began to count down from ten.

"Sabrina…" I mustered.

Without so much as looking in my direction, she spat back only two words.

"Fuck off."

The next thing I knew we were on the air.

Sabrina's venomous and angry face instantly turned into her award winning fake smile as she welcomed her viewers to *"the interview of this century."* However, as she launched into her opening monologue her expression became solemn and sad. She not only recapped the events of the tragedy in Honey Island Swamp but she read off the names of every known victim as their smiling faces appeared on the screen behind her.

It was a similar tactic to the one the prosecution had used in the courtroom during their closing statement, only this time there was the spectacle of a giant screen filled with faces of innocent people that were brutally murdered by Victor Crowley.

That's when Sabrina did something she had never done on television before.

She began to cry.

I recognized what she was doing immediately as it was the same fake cry that she had tried to master in an acting class she had taken in college. It's a simple tactic, really. All she did was hold her eyes open and not blink when she knew that the audience at home would only be seeing the victim's faces on their screens.

The whole thing was staged as once the red light on her camera was off a make-up artist ran in and gently smudged Sabrina's perfect mascara down her face as she silently blew what looked like an asthma inhaler into her eyes.

I was shocked.

The whole thing was one big production to paint Sabrina as a sensitive, caring talk show *hero* of some sort.

It also set me up to never have a chance at defending myself.

By the time the audience could see Sabrina on camera again her eyes were watering down her face.

I can admit that her acting skills had gotten much better since the last time I had seen her on camera. But when she faked getting choked up and pretended to collect herself I almost burst out laughing. Thank god I held myself together. If I had so much as giggled I know the producers would have immediately cut to me and I would have been even more screwed than I already was about to be.

In the almost decade since the interview took place I've often beaten myself up for not just calling Sabrina out on live television and telling the viewers what had just taken place behind the scenes. But at that moment I was still confident that I could win the fight. Even more importantly, I was still convinced that the stunt I was about to pull would actually work. Calling Sabrina out would only hurt my real mission of getting her back.

The sad truth is that even after watching her pretend to cry for the victims, I still loved her and wanted her back in my life more than anything. I suppose I justified it by reminding myself that she was merely doing her job, but goddamn did it hurt.

I knew many of the victims. They were my co-workers and friends. I watched them die in front of me. She didn't know a single one of them. She didn't watch them get torn apart. She hadn't been blamed for it all.

What did *she* have to be crying about?

Before Sabrina even introduced me she threw to a commercial break and her make-up team swarmed around her again, fixing up and re-painting the perfect, beautiful face they had just worked so efficiently to mess up with fake tears. They finished with time to spare and Sabrina and I waited out the last two commercials in absolute silence.

When we were back on the air it was as if someone had "dinged" a boxing match bell and Sabrina wasted no time before throwing the first punch.

"So, Andrew," Sabrina said. "Why did you do it?"

"Well, Sabrina," I smiled back. "As was proven in court, I didn't do it."

She turned to her camera and merely said, "*Right.*" It was something pretentious that she often did on her show and that I and many of her critics had always loathed.

I remained focused on my goal and rather than get angry with her, I let her and the world see just how hurt *I* was.

"How can you of all people, not believe me? How could you, my wife, even think that I would be capable of-"

"Ex-wife," she spat back at me.

She addressed her audience as if I wasn't sitting right there. "As everyone knows, I filed for divorce the moment accusations were brought against this… *man*."

I was reeling against the ropes and we were only seconds into the interview/fight.

Changing the subject as quickly as possible, Sabrina hit me with her next question.

"Just so everyone can hear you say it again out loud, who did murder all of those innocent people, Andrew?"

"Victor Crowley," I answered with my blood boiling.

Once again, Sabrina gave her signature pretentious look to her camera.

I cut her off before she could throw another punch.

"I don't blame a single person for not wanting to believe what really happened. I wouldn't believe it either had I not been there. But it's the truth. As the world saw in the trial, there was not a single shred of evidence showing that I carried out those murders." I said.

"You're not the first person to get away with murder through flaws in our country's legal system," she retorted.

I don't remember much about the remainder of that segment of the show. It was like being on trial all over again only this time the prosecution was my ex-wife, there was no courtroom protocol to protect me, and her gloves were off. All I could hear was my broken heart pounding in my ears as I instinctively slipped back into calmly reciting the same rhetoric that Manahan had rehearsed me to say if necessary during my trial.

When we went into the next commercial break the producers literally stepped in and walked Sabrina and I to separate corners of the stage. They wanted to make sure that any confrontation we had would only happen when we were live on camera.

As soon as the next segment began I pulled the stunt I had planned and that I'll never be able to live down.

Once we were live again I asked to speak.

"Sabrina, I didn't come on your show to go over the same semantics from the trial. Everyone knows what happened in that swamp and everyone knows I was found innocent. Can I please just speak from the heart? *Please?*"

For a split second, I thought I saw the woman I had fallen in love with behind her eyes.

"Go ahead," she said.

I got down on one knee before her.

"Stand up," Sabrina said, terrified.

"No," I responded. "I've literally lost everything over this. My life has been destroyed. But the only thing I still care about is *you*. I forgive you for turning your back on me, Sabrina. But now that I've been proven innocent… now that it's finally over we can go back to the way things were."

I removed her engagement ring from my pocket.

"Stop, Andrew." Sabrina sternly warned me. *"Stop right now."*

"No," I said. "I can't and I won't. I could have appeared on any show for my first interview after the trial but I only wanted to see you. I love you, Sabrina. Please come home. I'll literally die without you. I forgive you."

She looked at me with fire in her eyes.

"You forgive *me*?!" She almost shouted. "Never, Andrew. Not in a million lifetimes."

I couldn't hold back the tears.

"Now get back in your seat. You're embarrassing yourself." She turned back to her camera. "We'll be right back."

As soon as we had gone to commercial, Sabrina stood up over me. It was almost surreal to be staring up at her like that as she was entirely silhouetted by the stage lights. She looked like an angel.

I was too blinded to prepare myself for the slap across my face that she delivered with her right hand.

And my eyes were still closed from the slap when she spit in my face.

I ran out of the studio and grabbed a cab home. I had technically broken the contract, which stated that I had to finish the full thirty-minute interview.

Clearly they were more than happy with what they had already gotten out of me.

In the months that followed, my re-proposal was turned into over two thousand different memes online. I was ridiculed on every major media outlet and my embarrassing moment was parodied on several late night sketch comedy shows. I was now not just the most hated person in the world. I was also the most laughed at.

Somehow my lawyers were able to get "The Sabrina Show" to only re-play the interview one time and although it took months of work, the various YouTube videos of the interview have all been taken down through extremely threatening cease and desists.

Sabrina and I have not spoken since that day.

I have read that her live interview with me remains her highest-rated episode in the history of her show.

When I signed my deal for this book her producers supposedly made a very high bid to have me do her show again. I had my representatives tell them "over my dead body."

But hey, if they offer enough money I guess you never know.

Victor Crowley may owe me my life back but Sabrina Caruthers owes me my humanity.

***** ***** *****

Over the next few years, I did many more interviews and appearances on talk shows, radio programs, and other publicized events. Though they were always the same, nothing else ever went as horribly wrong as that first one with Sabrina and eventually I became numb to the snide comments and condescending questions. I learned how to be a punching bag in exchange for a paycheck.

The truth, plain and simple, is that the ordeal I lived through in Honey Island Swamp cost me everything I had ever made and that even a decade later I'm still paying off all of my legal debts. Nobody would hire me, not even the most basic fast food chain. So if someone wanted to pay me enough to sit before cameras or microphones and be blasted for sticking to my story I would always say "yes."

What else could I do?

Secretly part of me still hopes that after all of these years of telling my story perhaps someone will start to believe me.

Epilogue

There have been several versions of this book with this epilogue removed and then put back in and then removed again. Ultimately, however, I have nothing left to lose and if I'm going to tell the truth I'm going to tell all of it.

On March 23, 2011, I tried to kill myself. I swallowed what I had hoped was a lethal combination of the Xanax and Ambien my doctor has had me on since 2007. Fortunately, I couldn't even do that right and my body rejected the pills at some point after I had fallen asleep.

I woke up having vomited the pill concoction out and suffering from the worst hangover I thought anyone could ever experience. Realizing something out there must have been looking out for me I did the only sane thing I could possibly do.

I tried again.

Just a few days later on March 31, I swallowed down two fresh prescriptions, consuming at least double the amount as my first attempt. Once again I had the same result and somehow my body rid itself of the poison once I had passed out.

I'm not going to lie and say that I didn't consider a third attempt but fortunately for me, pills weren't going to work, I cannot get a gun, and I am too scared to do anything violent to myself like slit my wrists or leap off of a bridge.

But you know what?

These days I thank god that I didn't die from those pills. If I was supposed to die at the hands of Victor Crowley it would have happened that fateful night back in 2007 but for reasons I'll never quite understand… *I survived.* If I had taken my own life many years later it would have only been me finishing the job for him.

There are many nights when I actually pray that Victor Crowley will return. That I'll turn on the news and hear about a new unsolved murder in Honey Island Swamp like I used to hear about every so often over the years leading up to 2007. I certainly don't *want* anyone else to die but at the same time, if even just one more person could experience what I experienced in that swamp perhaps it would finally begin to validate what I have been saying for a decade now.

Hate me for saying it but if anyone else were to die in that swamp, they clearly never believed a word I said anyway.

It's just my luck that not a single incident or sighting has happened in Honey Island Swamp since the massacre, thus making me look like even more of a fool.

To add insult to massive injury, these days Honey Island Swamp has become a macabre and disgusting tourist attraction for twisted individuals wanting to see the scene of the crime and have "fun" scaring themselves with night tours of Victor Crowley's swamp.

In the years immediately following the trial Honey Island Swamp literally became an amusement park, complete with walking tours of the old Crowley property. I find it not only disgusting but extremely offensive to those of us who lost friends or family in there that the new property owners have memorialized the remains of the Crowley house and turned the shed into a makeshift museum that displays some of the actual weapons that were used in the murders and that were collected from the crime scene. Weapons that the forensic experts determined to have been used to commit the murders.

I would like to take this moment to remind you that it was proven beyond a shred of a doubt that not one of the weapons used in the murders contained a single fingerprint or hair follicle of my own. Hell, the six-foot-long chainsaw weighs over 125 pounds. There is no conceivable way that I could have possibly even held it up on my own two feet but for some reason, the world likes to ignore the facts of the comprehensive investigation.

The court of public opinion continues to claim that as an EMT who is trained in handling bodies and evidence, I would have known how to expertly remove my fingerprints and hair follicles from each of the weapons.

To that, I can only say… try it sometime, Geniuses.

Ten years later the hard facts still don't seem to matter.

As far as the prosecution's claim that DNA partially matching my own was found on two of the victims, I still don't have an answer or even a clue how that would be possible.

The victims were Asian males that also happened to be twin brothers and who worked for a chain of voodoo shops in the French Quarter. They were about eighteen months older than me so the best I can offer is that the DNA analysis was wrong or that the evidence was tampered with to try and frame me.

Either that or perhaps my parents never told me the truth about the miscarriage my mother suffered before they had me. Just maybe my mother gave birth to twin boys and gave them up for adoption fearing that she and my father were too young and too broke to provide the boys with a fighting chance. Maybe my estranged brothers also wound up in Honey Island Swamp that same weekend? You might laugh at that theory, but don't think I haven't considered it many times over the years.

Given that my parents never told me about my derelict cousin Bang until they absolutely had to, who knows what other secrets they had.

Unfortunately, I'll never have the chance to ask my parents if they were hiding something from me. But now that I've lived to see a monstrous ghost massacre dozens of people right in front of me I have no choice but to believe that absolutely *anything* is possible.

Every ghost hunting television show has done at least one episode in Honey Island Swamp. Two of them claimed to have captured audio of Victor Crowley's ghostly wail but I'm telling you once and for all that their findings were 100% faked.

I know what Victor Crowley's mournful "Daddy" actually sounds like. I hear it in my dreams nightly and I likely will until the day I die. The audio recordings on those shows sound *nothing* like Victor Crowley's voice because they're missing the most horrific element.

The element that only *I* would possibly know about being that *I* am the only living human being to have heard it and lived to tell about it.

Well, unless you count "Jane Doe."

The most chilling aspect of Victor Crowley's voice is that buried deep within it is a *child's* voice.

I heard it clearly.

I can still hear it now if I just close my eyes.

"Daddy..."

If I were to run into the devil himself it wouldn't scare me as much as that unholy voice does.

So where did Victor Crowley go? For all of the forensic work done in that swamp cleaning up the aftermath of the massacre they never found a trace of him anywhere and to this day there has not been a single incident in Honey Island Swamp. I only wish I had the answer for you.

Apparently, I had a front row seat to Victor Crowley's final killing spree.

Lucky me.

In my never-ending quest to prove my innocence, I have spoken to everyone from forensic experts to paranormal investigators to voodoo priests and not a single person has an answer.

There is one person however that I believe *might* be able to help me make sense of all of this. Unfortunately, he is currently serving out the rest of his days in prison for sexually assaulting a 12-year-old girl.

His name is Abbott MacMullin and he is the only living relative in the Crowley family. I couldn't tell you a single thing about Abbott as once I learned what he was incarcerated for I immediately abandoned the idea of ever speaking with him. I don't need to have any association with a convicted pedophile if I'm to ever clear my name, thank you very much.

Abbott is sadly the only living person who might possibly be able to validate the legend of Victor Crowley… and he's a fucking child molester.

Once again, just my luck.

At the time of this writing, business has started to slow down in Honey Island Swamp. Like any tragedy, time has begun to erase it from the zeitgeist and the morbid public has apparently moved on to wanting to visit the location of some other atrocity.

As for me, I haven't been back to Honey Island Swamp since the night I escaped. Just last Halloween I was invited to do a paid appearance at one of the swamp tours' "Halloween Swamp Nights" event. Though they were very clear that I'd only be appearing on the mainland and not required to go into the swamp itself, once I learned that the name of the tour company was "Crowley's Swamp Tours" I couldn't pass fast enough.

Every now and then I'll get an offer from some low rent television show to do an interview back at the scene of the massacre but no amount of money will ever get me back there no matter how desperate for cash I may be.

Recently "The Sabrina Show" has taken a massive hit in the ratings.

Last December Sabrina posted a tweet wishing everyone a Merry Christmas. Many years ago there would be nothing wrong with something like that but the current trend is for everyone to be offended by *everything* and the flavor of the month game is to ruin celebrity's careers.

By Sabrina *only* wishing everyone a Merry Christmas in her tweet she apparently excluded people of other faiths and (due to the holidays always being a slow time of year for the news) she found herself in the crosshairs of social justice warriors and being called a "racist." Although Sabrina's PR team immediately issued a heartfelt apology for her "ignorant and abhorrent" Merry Christmas tweet, the court of public opinion had already spoken and people began boycotting her show and petitioning the network and all affiliates that carry "The Sabrina Show" to drop it immediately. Much to my surprise, several affiliates have already dropped the show over the so-called insensitive tweet.

As her ex-husband and the man who likely knows her better than anyone else, I could tell you that Sabrina Caruthers is not a racist.

But why would I ever do that?

After all, the people have already tried and convicted her.

How does it feel, *Ex*-wife?

Unfortunately, I still love Sabrina despite all that she has done to hurt me. If you actually think a self-made African-American woman who married an Asian-American man of Chinese ancestry is a *racist*, you're an absolute fool. Sabrina may be a great number of things but "a racist" she most certainly is not.

You're welcome, Sabrina.

*****

Over the years I've heard of several films about the Honey Island Swamp massacre being developed. Some have been Hollywood studio movies but most are merely scrappy independent B slasher movies that either never got made or never got distributed. As soon as it was announced that I was writing this book I received several offers from various producers and production companies looking to option the rights to my life story but so far I haven't accepted one. I wish I could tell you that I've turned down the offers out of respect for the victims and their families. I wish I could tell you it's because I still have a shred of dignity left and do not want to see the tragedy or myself turned into what will inevitably be just another Hollywood horror film. The truth is that I've been advised that if I wait until after the book comes out the offers will increase dramatically.

To those who want to point fingers or shame me for what they claim has been me "cashing in" on other people's deaths over this last decade, all I can say is that I made peace with all of that shortly after society turned its collective back on me. In some ways, I have paid more dearly than the victims themselves for what Victor Crowley did in that swamp. I was wrongfully accused and wrongfully imprisoned for crimes I did not commit and that I too am a victim of. Even though the facts proved my innocence beyond a doubt, I will forever be wrongfully blamed for every single false accusation that was ever thrown at me. For the rest of my life, I will never be able to live in peace. I will never be able to seek employment or even leave my home without the fear of being assaulted both verbally and physically. I may have escaped with my life, but what kind of life is this when I can never again have the fundamental human rights I am entitled to as a free and innocent man?

My story and my *truth* are all I have left now that my life has been stolen from me. I am merely continuing to try and survive.

I ask you, oh righteous reader, what would *you* do?

As the tenth anniversary of the tragedy approaches, life has gone on for the rest of the world but for the families and friends of the victims (myself included) life has never been the same and never will be again. As I have expressed over and over again, my heart goes out to every single human being affected by Victor Crowley's murderous rampage. I only wish I could have saved some of them.

I did all I could.

Over the years I have attempted to connect with the families of my own friends and co-workers that lost their lives in Honey Island Swamp but all of my efforts have been ignored or painfully rejected. A constant reminder that even to those that knew me the most I will forever be considered the boogeyman.

In closing, I wrote this book not because I believe it will change anyone's mind about me or convince you to actually believe in Victor Crowley, but so that I can know that at least the truth now exists out there in my own words. I also wrote this so that people can know who I really am and what I've been through.

I did not commit any crimes.
I was found innocent.

It's on you, dear reader, to accept the facts or not.

Society has seen to it that I will always be blamed for the tragedy. That is the unfortunate cross I have to bare. Unless a tragedy is deemed "an act of god" there always has to be someone to blame and sadly that burden has fallen on me simply for surviving.

As we saw firsthand, even with Hurricane Katrina it only took a few hours after the rain stopped before the fingers began pointing at individuals and organizations that the country all felt could have done something to prevent the tragedy in the first place. It is merely how it goes in the human race, even when it's a natural disaster and only god is to blame.

While I cannot tell you if there is indeed a god, I can tell you that he or she does not exist in Honey Island Swamp.

Through the years I've learned to accept my place in all of this. Not as a victim but as a survivor.

A survivor of a massacre, a survivor of the ugly side of society, a survivor of myself, a survivor of suicide, and a survivor of Victor Crowley.

To anyone out there who is contemplating taking your own life, I won't try and tell you that I've had it worse and that you can, therefore, make it through. Depression is an illness, not a contest. We all face our trials and tribulations differently. What I can tell you is this:

As someone who has witnessed the kind of atrocities that no human being should ever have to see in their lifetime and as someone who has been treated so terribly that I sank just about as low as I believe a human can sink…I'm still here.

You deserve to be, too.

Talk to someone and think it through very carefully before you attempt something as careless and cowardly as I did. If I could go back I would heed my own advice but I wasn't in my right mind when I attempted to take my own life.

Then again, I'd imagine that anyone who would attempt suicide is certainly not thinking rationally either.

It may be easier said in hindsight but nevertheless I'm telling you that even I, one of the most unfairly hated men alive in the world today, am choosing *life*. It may always be a struggle, but I genuinely believe that if I can keep going then so can you.

The National Suicide Prevention hotline is open 24/7 and there are qualified people waiting to help you. Don't wait. Call.

1-800-273-8255

For those reading in other countries, I assure you that a phone number for you to call can be found in mere seconds online. Please, call before you do anything you cannot take back.

I still believe it can and will get better for all of us.

When this book comes out I will do one last round of appearances and put myself through the ringer of abuse one final time. The truth needs to be heard and if even just one person who reads this book finally believes me then it was worth writing. After that, I will do everything I can to move far, far away and try and start my life over again somewhere where just maybe I can be judged on the person I actually am.

Victor Crowley may have disappeared for the last ten years but I assure you that he indeed existed. With that once condemned swamp now filled with visitors almost nightly, I'd like to believe he is somehow gone for good.

I don't.

Victor Crowley is death itself and I don't believe that death can ever die.

So go ahead and watch the inevitable horror movies that Hollywood most surely has in store for us about this tragedy. Buy all of the "Victor Crowley Lives" garbage merchandise they peddle on Bourbon Street. Scare yourselves with ghost stories about him until you've had your fill.

But stay out of that swamp for I believe he will return.

Mark my words.

It's only a matter of time before it all happens again.

Acknowledgments

To my co-writer, Joe Knetter, thank you for at least pretending to believe me as we worked through this long process together. Thank you for your never-ending patience while guiding this retired EMT through the process of writing a book. I do hope we will stay in touch long after this book comes out.

To my new publicist, Kathleen, thank you for being brave enough to take me on as a client and for all of your help navigating me through the many, many wolves.

To Michael Manahan who defended me so stoically and to the jury that heard the truth and found me innocent, I owe you all my life. You know who you are.

To the Gibson family, please know that Randy was my closest friend. I miss him every day.

To the families of every victim, may you find the comfort and healing you each deserve. I hold nothing you've said about me against you and I have nothing but love and sorrow in my heart for each of you.

To my mother and father in heaven, I'm sorry that any of this had to happen. I will see you again someday… just hopefully not too soon.

Lastly, to the only love I'll ever know in my life, Sabrina… I forgive you.

IN THE DARK (Sabrina's Song)

Alone
So lost along my way
Cold
My lonely heart in disarray
At night
Close my eyes and you were there
In dreams
Always together somewhere

Living just for you
You are my dream come true

(Chorus)
Because I knew you before I met you
Loved you before I saw you
You've always been my one
You've always been my sun
Through the black of space and time
Your heart has always shined
You gave my life its spark
Ever since I held your hand in the dark

Fade
Our souls dissolved into one
Drift away
Each night I'd come undone
Mystery
Though your face I could not yet see
Forever
I always knew you were the one for me

Through the night your starlight shone
My angel has come home

(Chorus)

Guitar Solo

Living just for you
My everything come true

(Chorus 2X)

Lyrics by Andrew Yong

I, SURVIVOR. is based on characters and events created by Adam Green for the HATCHET film series. Originally featured in the fourth HATCHET film VICTOR CROWLEY, this book was brought to life by co-authors Adam Green and Joe Knetter. To learn more visit www. ariescope . com .

ADAM GREEN is an American screenwriter, director, actor, and producer best known for the films HATCHET (2007), HATCHET II (2010), HATCHET III (2013), VICTOR CROWLEY (2017), FROZEN (2010), and DIGGING UP THE MARROW (2014). He has written, directed, and/or produced 10 films to date and is also the creator, star, writer, director, and show runner of the television sit-com HOLLISTON. He created the production studio ArieScope Pictures with cinematographer Will Barratt in 1998. Originally from Holliston, MA he now resides in Los Angeles, CA. I, SURVIVOR. is his first novel.

JOE KNETTER is an author best known for the books TWISTED LONELINESS, VILE BEAUTY, ROOM, INSPIRED NIGHTMARES and ZOMBIE BUKKAKE. He has also written a number of screenplays that are in various states of production. Originally from the blustery cold of Rochester, MN he now resides in sunny Los Angeles, CA.

The authors would like to thank Parry Shen, Sarah French, Austin Bosley, Ashley Besh, Alejandro Cervantes, Casey Hempel, and Arwen.

37886120R00167

Made in the USA
Columbia, SC
01 December 2018